THE ATROPOS MAKER II

A NEW ORDER

A novel by **N.J. Lujan**

Publisher, Copyright, and Additional Information

The Atropos Maker II, A New Order by N. J. Lujan
published by https://www.njlujanofficial.com/

Library of Congress Control Number: 2020915829

ISBN: 978-1-7356246-0-0 Hardcover
ISBN: 978-1-7356246-1-7 Paper Back
ISBN: 978-1-7356246-2-4 E Book

Editing by Michael McConnell
Cover design and interior design by Rafael Andres

To my family and friends for their continued support since the beginning

To all the organizations that work determinedly and unselfishly to combat the atrocities like the ones depicted in this book in order to bring our children home.

To all the innocent children that have been stolen, you have not been forgotten.

No book is a single person's product. I am privileged that *The Atropos Maker II: A New Order* has benefited from the input of several great people.

My beta readers, proofreader, my editor, and Rafael Andres, my cover and layout designer, have been invaluable in shaping my book.

CHAPTER 1

Everyone OK? Alexander's fingers pound away at the phone's keypad. He hits send, then paces while clutching his cell phone tightly between his sweaty palm and fingers. *Mom confirm. Is everyone OK?* he repeats.

The grandfather clock's pendulum swings to and fro, leaving Alexander to wonder if his parents, Norma and Alex, are still "sufficiently capable." It has been five years since Norma, Alex, and Donovan rescued Alexander and the Atropos team out of the Lesser Caucasus Mountains. Norma and Alex, now in their mid-forties, find that the blade moves just slightly slower, and the bullet pierces just slightly off target. Alexander senses that, however still effective, they should back off and leave the dangerous missions to the members of the Atropos team. If they make it out alive, hopefully Norma and Alex will agree. Alexander bets not. As the previous director of the agency, Rick never carried out such missions. *Why are they?* Over and over and over, the question *Why don't they listen to me?* nags at Alexander.

This will be my fault. I should've been on that fucking helicopter, he thinks, *not stuck here at home.* He can hear his mother firmly, and quite clearly, order him to sit this one out. Bed rest was an absolute doctor's—and ultimately Norma's—order. There's no chance Norma is going to let this virus strain take out the born leader of Atropos. "Rest in a room at The World Renaissance Hotel so that the agency can take care of you, Alexander," Norma had said.

The World Renaissance Hotel, in the heart of Washington, DC, is as clandestine as they are and equipped to handle even viral assaults like this one on Alexander. Made agents and agency doctors tend to the government's most skilled covert teams that occupy these rooms. Norma was not pleased that he opted to stay home, alone. His strong-minded persistence was *her* running through his veins.

Alexander coughs, forcing some of the phlegm to loosen from his burdened lungs. Typically, one vial of agency-issued TRH (tissue-regenerated hormone) would do the trick, but this hungry superbug seems as resilient and deadly as Atropos, sucking the life out of Alexander. His tissue quickly heals, only to be attacked again. It will take an ordinary approach to kill this invader. An inhaler and prescription medicines have been his arsenals the past two days. "Mom, call me when you get this message," Alexander says to her voicemail. He tosses the cell phone onto the couch, wipes feverish sweat from his brow, then picks up his laptop to review the next mission. A distraction is needed. A vivid blue beam scans his eye and a hologram of Earth rotating quickly suspends in the air. Alexander navigates, swiping with his finger until the classified intel is received. He switches views and attempts to zoom in on them, still the screen blacks out. "NO VISUAL AVAILABLE" reads across the screen. Frustration runs wild as he slams the laptop closed.

Crisp air begins to drift through the open window of his penthouse apartment, giving Alexander a chill. He's not sure if its Washington, DC's fall air whisking passed him, or fear that his parents are dead that makes his body shiver. He shuts the window and drops back down onto the sofa. *Shit! Where the hell are they?* he thinks. Alexander falls farther back into the plush leather, restlessly waiting for her return call. He sighs, then calls again. "Come on, pick up," he mumbles.

He looks at the grandfather clock hands pointing to the fact that they are more than an hour past the pickup time. It is now 20:17. This was a difficult mission, and he can recall wishing, insisting for his parents to stand down. Norma and Alex chuckled at Alexander's worry. Let David lead the Atropos team, Alexander pleaded. Norma and Alex smiled, rejecting his worrisome chatter.

The cell phone rings once, and Alexander answers.

"Mom!"

He is relieved to hear her exhausted voice as Norma confirms that everyone is safely on the stealth helicopter. She provides their location's coordinates.

"I will call when we touch down," Norma says.

"You guys get some rest. I will see you soon," Alexander says.

"I love you, buttercup," Xavier says robustly, shouting, drowning out Norma's softer *I love you.*

"Will that bastard ever die?" Alexander says, breaking between a wheezing cackle, then a wet, rattling cough. "Tell

Xavier to shut the hell up!" The director has said Xavier, one of the three originals of Atropos, should be of higher station. If not for his humorous appetite and willingness to "kill them all, and let ole Saint Peter sort them out," as Xavier would say, he would be higher than third in command.

Alexander calculates their estimated time of arrival at The World Renaissance Hotel and contemplates whether he should join Donovan there to greet them. *Mom will kill me if I get off this couch*, he thinks, remembering the condition to stay home. Alexander stretches out on the sofa and sighs. He can rest now. The warm blanket is pulled up over his body, and his pale lids soon cover his hazy blue eyes that are streaked with red lines. Days of violent coughs and projectile vomiting have made his eyes bloodshot.

The darkness brings panic, and he abruptly sits up, awake. Alexander quiets his pounding heartbeat. For over five years, sleep has eluded him but for spurts—hours here, hours there. Norma trained him to command Atropos, but how to command haunting ghosts or stop visions of Ares' head rolling in front of him he must master himself—as she still tries to silence the banshees that haunt her.

He gets up off the couch and staggers to the bathroom, rubbing sleepy eyes. "Good God," he mumbles, looking into the small bathroom mirror as he straddles the toilet with pajama pants just slightly pulled down. He sees the red torrents streaking beside his cobalt eyes. His dark hair has a sheen of night sweat. The toilet flushes as water flows from the sink. His hands rinse as the wide vanity mirror offers a better view. *I look like shit,* he thinks. The cabinet below the sink opens and medicine is retrieved. He takes a swig and heads back to the couch. Soon his dreams replay in vivid color.

CHAPTER 2

"Alexander! Wake up! Open the door!" Norma's alarming voice penetrates the steel door, jolting him awake.

Alexander stumbles, rushing to the door, then quickly opens it. Norma's face appears stressed through the opening slit.

"What! What's wrong?" Alexander yawns. He tries to lift the fog that clouds his mind.

She pushes her way in. "No time. Get dressed quickly and come with me," Norma demands.

In Alexander's world he knows to replace measured words with action. He rushes to the bedroom as Norma hurriedly gathers his wallet, gun, and keys off the coffee table. "Hurry," she yells.

The passing minutes feel too long for Norma when Alexander finally meets her at the door. He turns back to lock it as Norma pushes the elevator button. "Shit," he says. Alexander turns the key back to re-open the door. Quickly he grabs the inhaler off the coffee table. Once out, the key is quickly pulled out of the door lock and the elevator opens. Alexander presses his hand against the digital panel that tenants use to count floors. This will take them one level lower than anyone in this building is privy to exit nevertheless see in the buildings as built—the contractors print on how it was constructed. Alexander made sure of that when ensuring Norma's esteemed engineer Daniel won the bid for renovating his penthouse. It was because of this that Norma was able to move as invisible as a ghost when thought to be dead. By Norma's alarm, Alexander knew the secret way out was essential for their exit out of the building.

The elevator doors seal shut, and Norma has a second to brief.

"Donovan has been trying to reach you. You have been compromised. We need you to get out of here until the threat is stabilized," Norma warns. If not for the med-induced sleep, he would have heard the many missed calls.

The fog lifts and his thoughts become clear. "Do we know who?" Alexander asks. His hand is pressed against the elevator wall and arm extended to brace his rundown body. A soupy, moist cough echoes in the confining elevator. "They couldn't wait until I feel better?" He smiles. "That's a punk move, picking on the sick," Alexander jokes, flashing a boyish grin to Norma.

Norma's fatigued eyes show signs of retirement in the near future. So Alexander hopes. Or perhaps just a very long nap is needed to rid the red lines streaking in her eyes. This is Norma's wish. After jumping in a different time zone and countless bloodshed left wetting the sand, she looks as rundown as Alexander. She smiles. The light catches dull red flakes in her raven hair.

"Are you hurt?" Alexander asks. He looks at her cheek and forehead and sees more blood speckling and smearing over her ivory skin.

"No. Stop fretting, son." She adjusts the gun tucked tightly into her firm waistband, then reaches for her back to shift "old trusty," to realign with the ridges of her spine. "I gave the guys my key to get into your apartment. They will stay there until further notice."

The elevator door opens to a corridor that will take them to the steps climbing up into a dark, secluded alley.

"Where are we going?" Alexander is working to catch his breath.

Norma gestures to the inhaler. "Take a puff now. We will need to move quickly to the Lincoln Memorial."

Alexander puts the mouthpiece to his lip and inhales deeply for two, maybe three seconds, then holds his breath as they rush through the passageway. A breath releases slowly from his lungs. "I can make it," he says. Cautiously, with Norma leading, they both quietly, slowly climb the stairs until they are assaulted by scents of dampened, rotting trash. Their eyes scan behind a row of Dumpsters shimmering from the moonlight, ensuring no one is around. Sounds of car horns and buses' airbrakes hissing from the other side of the building reverberate and bounce off the alley walls. As their feet move quicker, the smell of vomit overcomes Alexander, forcing him to taste again the chicken noodle soup Norma had made for him before deploying. His stomach is still suffering from days with the flu. "I think I am about to add to this wretched smell," Alexander says. It has been months since he has used this exit, and now he remembers why. At times, if returning with visible injuries, he would hide out at The World Renaissance Hotel until all was healed. Other times he took the gambit that people at the penthouse will believe his fabricated spin about dojo mishaps or mixed martial art death matches.

"Are you okay?" Norma asks.

"I can make it," Alexander says. He follows closely behind Norma as they disappear in rushing foot traffic. She blends with the night from the black clothes she is still wearing since her return. Only cars bright headlights beaming next to street lamps offer any visibility. Alexander, with head down, hunkers slightly behind her five-foot eight smaller frame. He is too tall to get lost behind her, but, if Donovan's intel is correct, visibility is not their enemy. Norma and Alexander know the sidewalks and streets are sparsely filled and a strike now would guarantee more boots would touch the ground as skis light in the terrorists' country. But then again, Rick did try to blow her up on the streets of Washington, DC, not too far from where they are now. Norma spots a creeping black sedan and nudges Alexander farther away from the street and deeper into a crowd of hurrying pedestrians rushing to a late dinner. Chills are running hard over Alexander as his aggravated lungs begin to wheeze over the brittle fall air.

"Not much farther," Norma says. She leads him through the National Mall until they spot the form of an ancient Greek Doric temple, the Parthenon. Norma always loved the Abraham Lincoln Memorial and its deep association to ancient

Greece, a tribute celebrating freedom for all. "Can you make it up the steps?" she asks as they begin to climb.

"*Now* who is the worrier? I can make it," he says, gasping. "You act like I'm on my last leg. My *TWO* are working just fine." Alexander follows closely behind Norma, wondering why she is taking them up the memorial's stairs only to land high up in the open as if tempting the sniper shot to be easily made. The shielding crowds have long dispersed to restaurants blocks away, and the lighted memorial spotlights them in the dark, yet he trusts her irrevocably, so he continues to follow. Norma stops, then stands where Lincoln sits. "Ummm, Mom. Is this a good time for sightseeing?"

Alexander watches as Norma looks down the empty flight of steps to where, if on foot, by the moonlight she would see them in this extraordinarily open space. The closest shadows she can detect linger by the Washington monument until her eye catches a moving figure to the right.

"Alexander! Behind the column now!" Norma motions for him to hide. He is too weak. She moves stealth-like down the opposite side of the stairs, then jumps farther left, avoiding the remaining steps. Her legs crouch and she positions to pounce. Across the steps she can see the man from the spotted sedan and recognizes him from previous intel. There is no doubt he is tracking up toward Alexander. They have been followed.

Norma stalks where the moon's luminescent light cannot reach. The gun is pulled from her waistband, and a bullet enters the chamber, ready. A suppressor is pulled from the compartment inside her jacket, then attached. Norma makes her move. Like a black panther, the strongest and deadliest in the kingdom, pouncing on its prey, her feet spring up onto the side of the stair she is silently creeping up. He turns with gun drawn toward her, firing. Norma can see the light whiz past her head. He misses. As Norma runs toward him, he runs down to meet her with a long-armed strike across her head. She ducks, then rapidly rises to return with an uppercut, precisely striking under his jaw. The heel of her palm strikes his forearm, then wrist making the gun release from his hand. It is an old battle protocol: first attack the arm that attacks you. Another strike against his face is delivered. His head jerks back, spurting blood like a red fountain while his hands reach, grabbing her body violently into his. He spins her so that her back can be forced tightly against his chest. His arms wrap forcefully, containing her for the moment he needs to finish her. Norma pushes the back of her body even harder against him as her foot kicks back to crumple his knee. Her hands quickly move to a low praying position, then drives them under his arms' tight hold. She pushes up high to the sky, freeing his body from hers. Disciplined adrenaline fuels the spin of her deadly feet with a roundhouse kick, then a chambered front kick. He mirrors her discipline and is equally savage. Unyielding, like the crescent moon, he squares his hips, pivots, and kicks, striking her chest. Her gain is lost as she loses balance and falls back onto the hard granite stairs. Air from her chest is knocked away as a rib can be heard cracking. Norma moves slowly to get up. He leans in to make the final blow. Her leg cocks toward her chest. She kicks him away, then returns her right leg close to her chest to pull the gun from her boot. She points and fires. His body falls forward, tumbling down the steps, leaving blood to cascade down after him. He lands next to where Norma lies. She confirms he is dead and that he was alone, at least for now. Norma is certain that whoever is remaining will meet the same fate as him if Alexander's penthouse is about to be breached.

Her feet barely touch every other step until she reaches the two Doric columns where Alexander has been hiding, prepared to defend.

"Follow me," she says softly, grabbing his cold hand. "Stay close." Norma takes Alexander directly beside where Lincoln sits. There is a break in two narrow walls next to the massive marble columns to the left of Lincoln. With no eyes but hers and Alexander's to witness, Norma reaches below Lincoln's hand and pushes on the fasces below.

"What is she doing?" Alexander mumbles as the inescapable desire to finish the several blocks to reach The World Renaissance Hotel has been stopped cold.

He continues to watch, intrigued, as Norma with one arm holds her ribs as the other pushes the fasces harder. She grunts.

The fasces (FAS-eez) symbol is that of a bundle of rods bound by a leather thong. In ancient times, fasces were a Roman symbol of power and authority, that a man held imperium. Most tourists believe it to be books carved into the Georgia white marble. Norma, being a Greece aficionado, understood the symbol well.

She uses more force until the screeching sound of marble scraping marble forces her to lose balance. She stumbles forward onto Lincoln's feet. To the left of Lincoln's grand statue the side walls shift back and apart, revealing a small opening.

Norma quickly slips between the two walls and stops, looking back at Alexander. "Come on. Hurry," she says.

Alexander squeezes between the two walls, then slides down a metal pole to the undercroft below, where the nineteen-foot Lincoln statue sits. He looks to Norma, then up to where he suspects Lincoln is. "Where does this go?" he asks, looking down the dark chamber. Alexander can feel the moistened ground below his feet and smell the mustiness from yesterday's rain. His lungs ache. The mouthpiece secures between his front teeth, and his lips close around it. A deep breath pulls the medicine into his lungs and is held.

"You are safe now," Norma says. They can hear the walls close above them. She grabs him and pulls him close for the chance to finally hug him. After Donovan had alerted her of his compromised status, she had been afraid. He was home alone and without the protection of his team. Norma rushed to be by his side.

Voices echo in the chamber.

Alexander draws his gun and points it into the darkness. Norma smiles and slowly nudges the gun to point down. "It's fine," she says.

"What, are you going to fucking shoot me, you douche bag," yells Xavier, clearly nearby. "I could've been home already with a clean ass and eating a big fat, juicy, USDA rib eye if not for your sick ass."

Alexander lets out a hearty chuckle, then feels and sounds to hack his lung up from his tender rib cage. As Xavier, David, Donovan, and Alex approach, Norma and Alexander walk to meet them. "Why in the hell did Mom pick you, the biggest, ugliest dumbass of the group?" Alexander says, playfully punching Xavier in his beefy chest. Xavier grabs Alexander in for a grizzly bear hug. "Good god, take a shower and shave," he says, pushing him away. "Pneumonia won't kill my lungs. Breathing in your foul lumberjack ass will."

"How are you doing, son?" Alex asks.

"You look like shit!" David pats Alexander on the back, then joins Norma's side. "So do you," he says, turning her face left then right to assess the damage.

"I'm fine," she says. "Nothing a vial won't fix!"

"Well, I feel like shit. I'm ready to get to the hotel and sleep!" Alexander says, then steps next to Donovan and raises his hand to shake. "Thank you." Donovan's cigar-stained fingers rise to accept Alexander's grateful hand.

"Anytime, kid. I'm just glad you're safe," Donovan says. Donovan turns to lead the way through the dark chamber. "With the intel we have, it won't be any time before you're back in your own bed."

"Where does this go?" Alexander asks. The chamber below the Lincoln Memorial soon ends and the dark narrow underground tunnel begins. Dim lights on the earthen walls barely light the way.

"This will take us to The World Renaissance Hotel," Norma says. "No one can find you down here."

Norma, Alex, and David take the lead as Donovan, Alexander, and Xavier follow.

Alexander looks to Xavier. "Exactly how many tunnels are there?"

"You know, even after twenty-five years, I really don't fucking know," Xavier says. Xavier studies Alexander, then looks forward at Alex. He notes their olive skin, black wavy hair, the muscular structure of their tall bodies, and can picture their identical cobalt blue eyes. “My god, in this dim light, you two could be twins.”

Alexander grins as he stares admirably forward.

CHAPTER 3

"Welcome, Mr. Alexander," Henry says. Slowly, his trembling hand reaches for the door to open with the same fondness as the five years passed since Alexander moved into these contemporary loft-style condos of the Penn Quarter in the middle of Washington, DC.

Alexander walks toward Mr. Henry, smile beaming, with renewed energy as his lungs take in autumn's melancholy air. The trees' lined down beauty strips have bid their leaves farewell. "Mr. Henry. How do you do?" he asks, rushing past him. It has been several days since he's been home. He is eager to surround himself with the comforts and quietness of his sumptuous apartment. Rude is not in Alexander's nature, so he stops, turns around, and engages to remind Mr. Henry that he matters. He takes a second to realize Mr. Henry's wrinkles have deepened, and his hair, like the late fall leaves, have all but fallen. What remains are white and silvery strands swept to the side. Unlike the seasons, new life will not spring vibrant in a short few months. Soon his will end, and Alexander will be greeted by a sprightly new face. Alexander sees a pin on Henry's uniform. "Is that new?" he asks.

"Yes, sir," he says. Mr. Henry straightens his concierge uniform with radiant pride. "It's a forty-year service pin. Only one ever to achieve it. I started here back in nineteen seventy-four." His sunken eyes, his thin lips, his kind spirit smiles at Alexander, warming him.

"Whoa, that's freakin' awesome!" Alexander touches the pin as if touching greatness. "Isn't it about time you retire? Enjoy some time with those grandbabies—hell, great-grandbabies—you keep showing me pictures of?"

"Oh, no sir. Ten more years on my mortgage," he says.

Alexander can't help but wonder if Mr. Henry's mortgage term has longer to go than Mr. Henry.

"Well, I better leave you alone. My apartment is calling my name."

"Have a good night, Mr. Alexander."

Alexander stops by a mail kiosk, then pulls overly stuffed mail out. A couple of days is common; several days has the slot overfed, bloated, looking ready to burst. Mr. Henry used to hand deliver until Alexander insisted that no special treatment was to be given. Current resident junk mail shuffles to the back as Alexander smirks at one that reads he is "guaranteed to win a million dollars." That he wishes for Mr. Henry. He can think of no other man more deserving. Alexander feels a presence, then the exotic scent of lily, jasmine layered with the woodiness of sandalwood, breezes past his nose. The allure overpowers him. He turns to see her standing next to him. Her pink nude lips pull back the curtain to reveal her brilliant smile. His heart flutters as he stares into her hazel eyes. What a strange feeling for someone not so easily unnerved. She can feel his energy, his warming attraction to her. Her eyes are forced to turn away despite a deep desire to look deeper into his soul. As she bends and retrieves a small package, he studies her shimmering long auburn hair and body that shows countless hours onstage dancing ballet. Her beauty instantly makes him an adoring fan. She raises as parts of him become erect, then a soft feminine giggle erupts. Alexander regains awareness that he has been staring admirably, lustily. "Oh, I am sorry. I don't know what's gotten into me. Hi, I'm Alexander," he says.

"Hi, I'm Nyx." A soft, delicate hand with pink, rounded nails and flawless skin rises to be lost in Alexander's tough, calloused hand. She flirts with yearning eyes, waiting for him ask her to dinner, coffee, anything, so that a future get-together was definite. Parting without would be disappointing to her. The heated energy between them was a mutually undeniable force.

"Alexander," calls out from David as he approaches, dispersing the chemistry that fills the hallway and reminding Alexander of agency rules.

"It was very nice meeting you, Nyx," Alexander says.

David is taken aback. "Nyx is your name?"

"Yes," she says, tempting Alexander to reconnect.

"Nyx was the Greek goddess of night," David says. He turns to Alexander. "Your mother would be amused. I can't believe I know that." David puts his hand on Alexander's back nudging him to walk with him toward the elevator. Alexander glances back grabbing a glimpse of Nyx standing rejected near the kiosk. He waves. She smiles. "You know the rules, Alexander."

"I know, I know. But damn, David. I have never seen a woman so beautiful."

"I know of one," David says, stepping into the elevator staring off with dreamy eyes.

"Oh my God, if you're talking about Mom... I'm going to vomit more than I did with that damn flu!" Alexander follows in and presses the penthouse button. "Everyone knows you are in love with her. Including Dad."

"Yeah, yeah, yeah. Let's just get upstairs and go over the next mission in two days. I figured you would rather do it at home than the agency."

Alexander's thoughts are still hovering around the kiosk. He wants to see her again but feels: *What is the point?* Still, he wonders; then he thinks of his parents' permitted marriage. *What would the leader of Atropos say?* he wonders.

CHAPTER 4

"All right, everyone. Listen up!" Donovan's voice overtakes the room, demanding all eyes and ears to focus forward. The Atropos team takes a seat as Norma and Alex stand beside Donovan next to the wood podium, watching and waiting. Alexander has already been warming the first chair at the front. David sits next to Alexander, observing the way his eyes slightly squint and face broods as he reads the pre-brief on his computerized watch for the mission ahead. David recognizes the resemblance from the days he sat in that seat and concentration was crucial. *Is the resemblance nature or nurture?* David wonders. Alexander breaks away from the screen on his wrist and looks up to see his parents alongside Donovan, standing where Rick once stood, to introduce him into Atropos. Even though over five years has elapsed, Alexander can still feel the rush of pride and joy overwhelming his body. Norma is alive, and his parents, along with Donovan, are the rightful directors of Atropos.

Donovan turns on the screen and begins with the first picture. A rundown follows of the remaining terrorist cells—who, when, and where in the Middle East they are hiding and the countries that are suspected to harbor them. Donovan displays the months of intel gathered and uploaded as the Atropos team securely download into highly precise memories in no time. Norma proceeds with profiling each member of the cell. She points out the slightest of movements, exposing their weak points, from previous injuries all the way down to a dominant hand or lesser-trained muscles. Alex continues with his portion on topography, demographics, and what they will need to be prepared for. Most of which is very common for this Atropos team. There is not an ocean that these men have not crossed. North and South Atlantic, Indian, North and South Pacific, and even parts of the Arctic Ocean's waves have crashed against borders that they covertly crossed undetected.

"The attempted attack here on Alexander is tied to this cell," Norma says. Donovan hands her the remote, and she turns slightly to face the large screen. A picture of the man she killed at Lincoln's Memorial shows on the monitor, then the two killed in Alexander's apartment are laid out side by side. It is a display of who was once on America's most wanted list but are now dead. Next an older face with a likeness to the man Norma killed comes next. "He is the father of him." Norma points to the first picture. "He was part of the original terrorist cell that charged into Iraq killing men and enslaving Christian women and children. He is responsible for many children being sold into human trafficking and continues to recruit for attacks on American soil. "It is your mission to capture him, extract information, and then exterminate him. He went after Alexander's head and failed… now it's my turn." Alexander watches as Norma uses the remote to blacken the screen. "Make it quick, make it stick," she says, then turns and leaves the podium with Alex and Donovan following close behind. They both exit as the Atropos men rally. "Hooah," repeats loudly, boldly with open lungs.

"Now this is as it should be," Alexander says. He steps into the elevator inside of The World Renaissance Hotel. David, distracted by thumbing a text before the signal drops, stalls for a second to hit send, then steps in behind him. "Mom and Dad need to lead from the agency office. Not charging a field."

"Alexander, you do realize your mother and I started at the same time? We're the same age. So is Xavier." David playfully shoves Alexander farther into the elevator, then turns, waiting for the beam to scan, approving their ride up. "Are you saying I'm too old for this shit now, too?"

Alexander scans David up, then down, as a beam scans them with the same motion. "Well, now that you mention it." A chuckle erupts. "I think we sleep here as much as we do at home," Alexander says. "I've had this same damn hotel room as long as I've had my penthouse." Alexander bumps his six-foot frame against David's five-foot-eleven body. "Are you shrinking, old man?"

David bumps back, putting Alexander in his place, and the two laugh. "Do you want to switch rooms?" David asks. "Need a little strange in your life? Maybe something new? Maybe by the name Nyx?" David throws words at Alexander to silence his notion that he and Norma are no longer "sufficiently capable."

"Oh good God. Please tell me that you did not tell Mom or Dad about Nyx," Alexander says. "I don't want to go home one day and find out from Mr. Henry that Nyx was evicted for some bogus HOA violation. That her forwarding address is somewhere in fucking Zimbabwe."

David is amused by the sweat on Alexander's brow. "Relax, son. Your mother does not know."

"I don't even know her. We've met once," Alexander says.

"That was some thick chemistry at that mail kiosk for just once," David points out.

Rather the combination of gravity and the tension in the cable or just recalling the feeling he felt at the kiosk, Alexander feels weird, his legs weakened as the elevator stops.

"Have a good night, gentlemen," Donovan's voice streams from mirrored panels as the elevator doors open.

Alexander's eyes widen and mouth gapes. He looks to David and mouths, *Fuck! I forgot he was listening. Great!* David is wildly entertained. In his time, he has never forgotten.

CHAPTER 5

Norma and Alex enter Donovan's office at the agency, and despite the many comings and goings, Norma can still feel Rick's troubled spirit in this room attempting to return to reclaim his seat. It was here that the devil's breath took him away. They sit in the chairs in front of the desk as Donovan readies the screen to check in on the Atropos team's arrival. "Let's see if our children have arrived," Donovan says. Their eyes identify each body through Alexander's third optical; funded and stamped AGENCY ONLY. Alexander, David, Xavier, Lander, Kosmo, Stephen, Raiden, Vali, Milo, and Nick—all ten—are all accounted for.

"What the fuck is Xavier doing?" Donovan says.

Norma leans in and studies the monitor. "Idiot," she smirks, watching as his burly figure trots in front of Alexander, sashaying, then adds: "Is he… twerking?" She watches as Alexander warns Xavier to walk the line, then David handing out a head slap. The men's smiles beam across the screen. Xavier was always good for settling down jumpy nerves. Norma tries to recall whether she has ever seen Xavier completely unhinged. A tear escape his eye? She thinks not, nor ever.

Norma, like Alexander, cannot sit idle on the sidelines and watch. She stands and begins to leave. Alex rises, adjusts his coat and tie, agreeing with Norma. "Call me if anything goes wrong," Norma says. Donovan ends the transmission for now and shuts down the computer.

"This is not a tricky assignment. Alexander and David can lead this team easily. Are you guys hungry? We can go down to Big Lou's Diner for the best fat, greasy cheeseburger in town."

"Donovan, how the hell do you eat that shit every damn day and stay so fit and skinny?" Norma asks. Norma looks to Alex. "Do you want to go?" she asks. "I'm sure that place has something other than a pounded cow rump or onions dunked in beer batter and swimming in oil."

Donovan smiles and leads them out the door, only turning around to protect it with the retinas of his eye. "You know changing this from a hand to an eye scan only means now that someone will lose an eye if ever kidnapped and breeched. I'd rather lose a hand than be stuck with just one shitty view. I need both to see the shitty shit we deal with." He pulls out a Cuban cigar for the four-block walk to Big Lou's Diner, then trails slightly behind Norma and Alex.

A white smoky cloud twirls, blowing in the rear offending the noses behind him. Scarves convert to masks as disapproving sighs sound forward. Donovan, not caring who is behind him, grins as Norma walks in front. He spots one long grey strand in her raven hair as she walks with perfect posture in two-inch heels mindful of cracks in the sidewalk. At forty-five her skin, like the fine tailored suit she is wearing, is flawless, without a single wrinkle. The white and mystic blue of her eyes still look as young and fresh as the threads on her body. Yet now Donovan sees proof that even *she* can't escape father time. He fondly remembers the young, insolent Norma that he did so well to protect. Bony cheeks rise and his smoke-stained teeth appear between thin, cracked lips. Her hair sways and the scar from the explosion tells the tale of the day their relationship was forever changed. A day Donovan came out from the shadows to save her. His eyes lower to the ground as he closely follows, then silently he let's go a warm, full-hearted sigh. The past five years have been incredible. Maybe if not by blood, this was the family, perhaps even daughter-like, he could have. His cranky heart smiles. Not quite the old bastard, bogus of an agent, Norma once thought him to be.

The three perch up at the bar where Donovan's favorite waitress, Elizabeth still serves him. Her apron over the years has expanded to encircle her waist. Whether from her son Charlie, born four years ago, or finding comfort in the food she serves Elizabeth has filled out since Donovan first met her. Her sunken tired eyes look to Donovan as she attempts to deliver an expected wisecrack.

"All this time I thought your 'friends' were a figment of dementia," she says. "Does the home know you snuck out again?" Without words, she turns to put in Donovan's usual order. "And how is it your friends look like they stepped out of a *HUGO BOSS* magazine and you look like you stepped out a Sears Roebuck catalog circa 1950?"

Donovan grumbles back as Norma and Alex grin at the jabs crossing back and forth over the counter as Elizabeth writes what they can only suspect are encrypted letters to the cook on how and what to prepare. "Now who is the cantankerous old person here? What's gotten into you lately?" Donovan pries.

"My son's daycare was shut down, so I had to find someone quickly to watch him while I work. The woman I found on short notice was a lot more expensive, so I had to pick up extra shifts to pay her," she says, then pauses, staring into the salt shaker. She hands it off to Donovan for him to shake the sea salt out like a wintery blizzard falling, blanketing his fries. "But I found someplace a lot cheaper." The words bounce off Donovan and return to Elizabeth, causing her to try to shake doubt as Donovan shakes the salt shaker. "Well, I don't know… The kids looked scared." Optimism builds, trying to reassure her. "I did meet the guy who owns it, and he seems really nice. Charlie—" Elizabeth glances over to Norma and Alex "—that's my son, did seem skittish around him. But Charlie is like that with strange men. You know, not having a daddy and all. And it's not like the men I've dated have helped his self-confidence." Then, just like that, optimism runs out with each word that parts her lips. "I don't know. I guess we'll see as time goes." Elizabeth abruptly stops and leaves her compelling story at the counter as they begin to eat. Donovan struggles to digest Elizabeth's explanation for her somber appearance. He wants to pry but isn't keen on overstepping boundaries. He prefers boundaries.

Norma, Alex, and Donovan rise from the barstools and Donovan reaches for the check. He invited so he pays: that's his rule. Norma and Alex oblige; only Norma insists on paying the tip. Donovan and Alex look down at the counter with approving eyes. Norma's bill was five times what Donovan's was. Donovan pats Norma's back. "I think that tough exterior is getting soft in your old age," he kids.

As they step onto the sidewalk, the sound of brakes screaming and tires skidding on the asphalt close by while pedestrian rush to move out of the way stop them at once. They pull guns from their waistbands then slide one in the chamber, ready. The building wall is used to cover their backs. The guns scan through the panicking crowd that is dispersing, afraid. This time paranoia is not their reality. This time muscle memory will prove to be correct. Three Arab men come into view carrying automatic weapons pointed at Norma, Alex, and Donovan. Three automatic pistols, each carrying thirty-three rounds, stand against the three automatic rifles. The insurgents stop several feet away, waiting for one to be fired. Despite the size difference, the massacre will be all the same. Norma can feel the innocent bodies all around at risk. Alex softly mumbles and gestures. "The underground entry in Big Lou's?"

Donovan quickly signals no, then whispers, "After you used it, we sealed it. There is a new entry to the underground tunnels one block east of here. It's inside one of the dressing rooms at Lavicci."

Norma takes a step out from Alex and Donovan toward the three beefed up men. Their clothes, their bodies, the committed warrior look on their face could be used to describe her Atropos men. Foreign faces with the same form of conviction—carrying out a vow to their leader, she thinks, then immediately reminds herself that her men would never use the children nearby for cover. "Cowards," she mutters. Norma removes "old trusty" from its sheath that's been routinely strapped on her back. She embraces the intimacy the knife offers. A sinister smile flashes on Norma's face as she entices: one, two, three… make your move.

A single round fires, then a grunt as hot lead shatters apart the thin skin and muscle Donovan has to shield his lanky bones. Fragments of his femur can be seen splintering out of bloody, gaping flesh. Lucky for him the bullet misses an artery. Donovan goes down, then uses his hand as a tourniquet to wrap around his wounded leg. Blood seeps up from between the cracks of his fingers. Norma steps in front of Donovan, guarding, as Alex steps to the side facing the three men. Alex looks to Norma. If they are to run, firing, some of them will die. Or perhaps, they may die…Donovan for certain. Innocent people for certain. A second passes, then Norma slightly raises her hands to gesture that they will come willingly. This is obvious; by the sum of bloodshed, that this was to be the terrorists' mission. Soon their leader will know that it was a success. Norma wishes she could learn a similar fate about her men. Is the Atropos team on a helicopter and arriving shortly? She expects soon they will learn of their disappearance in the light of the day on the streets of Washington, DC. She is counting on it. If not, they are not the only teams to check in at The World Renaissance Hotel.

Norma, Alex, and Donovan are shoved into the back of the blackened sedan, then squished together by the cold steel of rifles and bodies. Norma rips the tail of her shirt and removes Donovan's belt to wrap his leg. This might buy him time if he doesn't bleed out before this plays out. Norma notices he is becoming paler than normal. His eyes meet hers, and the tenderness of her expression encourages him to hang on. She reassures him that a little time is needed to get them out of this.

CHAPTER 6

"Who are you with?" Water splashes into Norma's face as she, Alex, and Donovan hang from a scaffold with hands and feet bound by handcuffs. Norma's eyes abruptly jerk open to see through the slit of her swollen lids that their captors want more than their bodies will be able to take. She feels confidence that the force that drives her mind will survive longer than the physical damage her body will suffer. Norma efforts to search the old abandoned building, then tries to calculate the time it took them to arrive. It takes seconds before she is certain of their location. Vacant due to a bankrupt industrial company, dusty metal hanging, trash left by vagrants seeking shelter, she spies and remembers seeing it televised. Another agency group seized this building two months back from drug traffickers. She saw it one morning while sipping coffee as the six a.m. reporter questioned loose-lipped agents.

"Tell us," he demands. "I'm losing my patience, Norma. Who is your team with? Where are they?"

Norma drives certainty deep into his mind: she will not break. She turns her head to the left to see what she hopes are Donovan and Alex looking back. Both have suffered the same pain. Their face and bodies pounded, ruptured, with feet sopping in a puddle of blood. Once freshly pressed suits are now serving as clinging bandages that are seeping. Donovan is barely hanging on next to her as he uses his left leg to balance as his right femur hangs, splintered out from his body. Alex looks past Donovan to Norma. He gives her strength. Norma looks to the one in charge. He was not there at Big Lou's Diner, but she has seen him before. She is certain. He is American with Caucasian roots, if she had to profile a Northerner who grew from a branch within our government. She senses military or agency quality. Norma can tell that Donovan and Alex feel the same sense of acquaintance and are raring for a chance alone. If Donovan's hunch is correct, it was five years ago at The World Renaissance Hotel.

He has Norma removed from her bounds, hands and feet now free. "Bring her to me," he says. Norma is dragged to stand in front of him. "I've heard so much about you." He closely circles Norma, hovering like a buzzard ready to shred her poised flesh. "You're not so scary." With her knife in his hand, he slowly taunts her that in any second, she will feel steel pierce her body. It was less than a second. She grunts, then stands, undaunted, as the knife just passes by a vital organ. "You really are beautiful." He uses her wet knife to rip her shirt, bra, and old trusty's strap from her body, exposing her breasts and upper body. Norma throws her shoulders back, then straightens her spine.

Norma forms a menacing smirk, stabbing him with the only weapon she has left. She hears Alex and Donovan struggling to get free, frantic to stop what is sure to happen. He gestures to the two armed men from Big Lou's Diner to control Alex and Donovan. *Now,* he silently demands. They sling their rifles as they walk off, then return with a pair of two-sided Heretic Forks with collars. The forks are tightly strapped around Alex's and Donovan's neck, forcing their eyes to stay straight on Norma. If their heads move again, four sharp spines will pierce their necks—two near the chin and two near the sternum. A medieval torture still proven effective in the country that commissioned them.

He presses his sweaty body against hers, then deeply breathes in her defiance. His chin touches her cheek as his body moves in even closer. She can feel his foulness poking her. He whispers in her ear. "This is going to be fun." He steps back to face her. His eyes travel down to her pants as his calloused fingers move down the center of her firm breasts, then stomach, then stop at her waistline. "Where is your team? Give me all of their names." His rough finger insults, sliding under her pants and her panty's waistline, slithering in and out. "Where is Alexander?" Norma can feel him agitate as she defies his ruse to incite fear. "You don't know me, do you?" At first she ignores, then chooses to look him in the eye.

Norma can hear Alex behind her, grumbling as if awakened to who this man is. Time has changed him almost unrecognizably. He disappears from Norma's sight as the two guarding men dare her to turn around. They are eager for their turn. She listens as his steps stop in front of where Alex and Donovan hang, bound with the fork spines beginning to puncture their flesh. Alex grunts louder as the fork buries deeper into his neck and sternum.

"Hello, old friend," the man says.

"Chris Logan," Alex grunts, finally seeing the traitor who once wore the same pin—*De Oppresso Liber* (Latin, "from an oppressed man to a free one")—while a Special Forces sergeant in the Army.

"Did Alexander tell you we met? I heard about the quaint little family reunion in the Lesser Caucasus." He shouts back toward Norma, "You should've stayed dead! You should've let us kill Alexander." Logan shifts focus, moving to where Donovan struggles to keep his head up. Donovan is growing weaker by the second as the shattering pain and blood loss from his beaten body render him defeated. Soon the forks will disappear into Donovan's neck, and cold, silent grayness will hang. Logan removes the belt from Donovan's leg, then takes the tip of Norma's knife and slides it in under a bone fragment sticking out from Donovan's mangled flesh. His fingers push deep into Donovan's flesh, stopping at the knife's tip, coating with dark congealing blood. He takes hold of the fractured piece of bone and pulls it farther out of Donovan's leg. Donovan's head and back arch backward as he screams when the piece of bone is snapped off then pulled free from his body. Logan takes the jagged piece of bone and returns to Alex, leaving Donovan's body to tremble as his head bobs. Donovan no longer feels the pain as the fork penetrates deeper into his neck.

"You three really pissed some people off. That was my boss you killed five years ago." He takes the sharp bone and runs it down Alex's neck, splitting his stretched skin. Alex's blood mingles with Donovan's blood that coats the jagged bone. Alex's veins are popping as the muscles in his neck flex to keep his head still. Square edges of the handcuffs dig into his wrist as he tries to use the strong force from his arms to split the steel apart. Norma can hear the metal clanking together as Alex fights to break free. "Bring me the prod. Let's see what fifty thousand volts does to this pretty face. Even better, drop his pants. It's time for a little foreplay."

"Now I see why you went over there," Norma yells. "You need a prod to do your dirty work. Is your dick really that small?" *Insolence makes her dangerous,* she once heard Donovan say. Norma turns around to face him. Logan gestures to the guards to stand down. "What's wrong, big boy, can't finish what you started over here? Bring that rod over here. Maybe then I can feel something. She looks to his crouch and scowls. "Aw, did it never grow to a real man's size? Is that why you left me over here?" She baits him to her. "Let me profile this. Bed-wetter until twelve? Daddy shoved his boot up your ass so many times it left you feeling gay? Perhaps the women with the misfortune to fuck you left you feeling inadequate? Norma looks up and down the beefed-up guards. "I can see why you switched teams. Takes less to fill those tight asses." She steps forward to meet him, pulling the baited line in closer as he rages toward her. "You're a fucking coward. A traitor! Was it money? Or was it because your incapable ass couldn't make it at the agency?" Logan violently moves forwards and swings his backhand across her mouth, knocking her off her feet. Norma quickly rises, wipes away the blood running from her opened lips, then rejoins the faceoff. He once again slowly circles her, breathing fire down her neck. Norma turns her back to Alex, enticing Logan's attention to remain on her as Donovan begins to awaken just in time to witness the terror.

"Oh yeah, I'm gonna have fun with this," he says. "Alex, watch this. I'll show you how to make your woman scream." He looks over to the guards. "If they look away, shoot them," he says.

Norma raises her hands, mocking, as to tease his ravage to penetrate her. She welcomes the darkness like an old foe that she refuses to allow to steal her virtue, her courage, her spirit, as it once did. She straightens her back even more to stand tall. Her bare breasts rise high. His hand rears back, then slaps her across the face, forcing her to lose balance. Her brain throbs from the impact. The two men standing nearby grab and place her back in front of him. She positions herself so that there is more distance between her and the guards. She can take one, maybe two, but all three may kill her.

"That's why I thought you needed that prod. You hit like a pussy. Twice and I barely felt a thing." Her pants are pulled down to bind her ankles, then her panties are cut off. He spins her naked body around and forces her to slightly bend forward. Logan grabs and holds the back of her neck firmly. Donovan looks past them, refusing to accept what he knows is going to happen. Alex flails side to side, flipping while wrestling the handcuffs, trying to break free. Her eyes widen, seeing the horror take over Alex as adrenaline races, wanting to stop it before Norma is raped of her dignity. Norma stares deep into Alex's eyes until she touches his soul, hypnotizing him to calm before he is silenced. "Show no emotion" deeply embeds that all cannot be taken. She compels him and soon all that is around them fades. She mouths: *Amica mea* (My love), giving Alex the strength to endure. For the moment, they are back to when they first met, then the hospital where they first became one.

Logan's pants open. The only weapon he is certain to shut her mouth is pulled out. Norma prepares herself as Alex's eyes never break from hers. The guards can be heard laughing, rousing for their turn. Before Logan's first thrust, Norma frees a foot from her pant leg, then slams against his body to release his hold from her neck. She spins behind him, then grabs his body against hers to shield her from the bullets discharging from the guards' rifles. She shoves Logan into the two guards and uses his back to launch her over them. She turns around, grabbing one of the rifles, then shoots three rounds into them. Their bodies fall together. Norma grabs the keys and unlocks the handcuffs that bound Alex, then frees the fork from his neck. Alex grabs a rifle, ready if more is to come. Norma quickly pulls her pants back on, then covers herself with her ripped shirt. She walks over to where Logan's body lay on the cold wet floor and reaches down. "That's what I thought. A dead fuck." Without delay, old trusty and she reunite. She uses the knife to slice the pale weapon Logan was so eager to use, then places it in his mouth. "Here. Not tonight. Your bitch slap gave me a headache. Now satisfy your fucking self," she says, then wipes the knife clean on his shirt.

"Donovan!" Norma calls out. She runs to his side, sickened that she may be too late. The fork is removed from his neck, and his hands and feet are set free. He slumps onto her. She carefully eases his body to the ground. "Donovan, you old bastard. You better not die on me." Donovan's eyes open, seeing Norma fretting over him. With a frayed piece of her shirt she rips it off, then wraps his leg tight. The belt is taken from the ground and re-strapped. "I don't think a band aid will save you from this one." Donovan smiles, remembering so many years back when her sarcasm secretly delighted him.

"Norma," he calls for her to come closer. Donovan feels time has run out for her to know. "You need to know." Norma leans down to listen. "Your dad and I were in the same unit… I've known…what they did to you."

Norma hushes his guilt. "Ssshhh," she whispers.

Donovan feels his chance slipping. The words fight being silenced as his mind fades. "I am sorry, Norma. I should've stopped them. You were a little girl. Not an experiment. What Rick did to you… you need to know about Alexander…about you." A teardrop falls down the crevices of his bruising, bony cheek. Loose, aged skin folds over bloody creases. Norma sees his frailness, not the strong, lanky old man she has grown to love. His breath labors to fill his lungs.

"You are not going to die here!"

"Let's get out of here," Alex says. "We don't know how many more there are or where the third one from Big Lou's is."

"Leave me," Donovan says. "Alex, get her out of here!"

Norma refuses to leave him to die alone. "I am not leaving you. This is my fault. If you had not helped me save Alexander, they would have never known you existed. I'm not leaving you."

"Go," he says.

Norma can feel her blood rush, making her heart pound as the wells of her eyes fill. She can feel his body beginning to give up. She can't watch this. She hesitates to get up but knows they need to move. Norma looks at him, defenseless, then rejects. "Hell no! I'm sorry, old man. You saved me once, now I'm saving you. Now we're even. Besides we're family, you stubborn asshole. I'm taking you out of here." Donovan's wobbly six-foot stature forces them to stumble as she helps him to his feet.

Alex rushes away from the still bodies to help Norma pick up Donovan. "I got this," he says. A tender smile, happy that this is over and she is safe, comes across Alex's face. The torture they endured doesn't compare with the torture he went through when he thought he had lost her. He could not take losing her again. His heart could not suffer that. His eyes tell her that he is ready for them to go home, ready to wrap her in his arms, ready to embrace her, ready to heal her. His love for her was insurmountable and only grew stronger over the decades. Norma sighs relief, ready herself to be alone with him, to heal each other. She returns his tender smile that radiates love for him. Alex reaches Norma and Donovan. "I got him," he says as his hand reaches out.

A round fires off, blaring in the hollow building. Alex's body and expression freeze. His eyes enlarge and his hand drops. He falls forward onto Norma and Donovan, knocking them over.

Norma frightens, needing a second to absorb what just happened, then she howls. "No!" She grabs the rifle from Alex's hand and shoots the guard who was thought to be dead. Quickly she returns to Alex.

Alexander and the Atropos men rush in, seeing that the intel was given to them a minute too late.

"Dad," Alexander yells, running to his side.

"Alex!" David charges in, then Xavier.

"What the fuck!" Xavier begins to madden.

Norma turns Alex over to see him gurgling blood. "NO! NO! NO!" She places his head on her lap as she wildly cries, begging for him to be okay. "Alex!" She can see the bullet's damage as his severed heart gushes his vital fluids out of the exit wound, spilling around them. She is in disbelief. "NO! NO! NO!" Her hand panics, quickly and unsuccessfully trying to plug the hole. She rocks back and forth with his head in her lap as her hand holds his heart. She leans against his head and breathes in his essence. "Alex," she continues to call for him. "Please!" Alex's eyes fight to focus as he looks deeply into hers, embracing her soul one last time. Calmness comes over him. "*Amica mea*," slowly escapes his parted lips with one last breath. She watches as the life leaves his eyes. Uncontrollable fear and pain runs down her face. "Alex!" She begs for him to look, look at her. She shakes him to awake, then leans in and desperately presses her lips hard against his, hoping to restore his life. "Don't leave me! Oh my god. Please don't leave me! NO! NO! NO!"

Alexander looks down, helpless. Tears fall for his father. Tears fall for his mother. He sees her panties on the floor, making his nerves jump out of control. He runs to the dead bodies and shoots at the thought of what just happened, until any trace of being is gone.

"Alexander, stop," David says. He sees the penis in Chris Logan's mouth and can only imagine what they had endured.

Alexander returns to Norma. "Mom." He reaches down to pull her up. She shrugs him off, then places her shattered body next to Alex, cuddling him, uncaring that his blood is now covering her face and body. She runs her red soaked fingers through his black wavy hair, then her arm drapes over him like so many nights before as she begins to drift. Her head rests on his shoulder as she clings tight. "*Amica mea*," she whispers in his ear. "Wake up," she softly begs.

Donovan stresses on all fours, exerting any remaining strength to get his feet under him. "Norma," he calls. "Look at me." He limps over to her, reaching for her arm. "Come on, my girl, you need to let David get him out of here." David comes to her side and leans down to pull her up. She can't leave Alex. Her arm returns to him and she kisses him, not wanting it to be the last.

"Mom," Alexander calls as the loss of his father overwhelms, and composure begins to be lost.

Norma can feel the last thread that is keeping Alexander together is about to break. She slowly rises, then falls deep into David's arms. "Give him a vial," she pleads. "TRH will heal him."

"I'm sorry," David says as he finds the strength to hold her up. David signals for Xavier and the Atropos team to surround Norma and Alexander as he takes their fallen Atropos man home. He orders Raiden to collect everything as he reaches for Alex, lifting his dead body into his arms. "*Donec mors nos separaverit*," he whispers (Until death separates us).

CHAPTER 7

David steps next to Alex's suspended coffin that has been draped with the American flag. The red, white, and blue complement the cobalt blue steel that Norma had picked, feeling it to complement Alex's sealed eyes. Norma, Alexander, Donovan, and Atropos stand, encircling the gravesite near Washington, DC.

Alex was an only child, and his parents died in a car accident shortly after he entered the military, making him the ideal candidate for a Special Ops team, then Atropos. Alex never knew if other branches existed, and once meeting Norma, he never cared. She was all he ever wanted. In less than an hour the dirt bed six feet below will accept Alex as his final resting place. Norma stares down with desolate eyes at the bed wishing to trade their lush bed at home and join him here, to lie next to him for eternity. Her blank expression tells everyone present that her soul is as black as the clothes she is wearing as she mourns Alex. When asked about military honors Norma felt there could be no one but Atropos that could deliver the respect Alex deserved.

"I feel it an honor to be here to say a final goodbye to our fallen warrior. I met Alex many decades ago when he was pulled in to aid in a rescue mission to bring back our leader, Norma. My first instinct was: Who is this guy? Is he capable? How is it that he is helping Atropos yet not part of the team? It was that rescue that changed many of our lives forever. When I stood next to him, I knew I was standing next to greatness. Greatness that would take me to her, only to later take her away from me, leaving me with no chance to win her heart." David's warm smile does nothing to thaw Norma's frozen stare. "But that is how it was to be. The love I witnessed between those two and the love they have for their son was inspiring. We did not just lose a heroic warrior. We lost a husband, a father, a best friend. A man who was comfortable serving in the background for the good of others. A man who protected our country with the same dedication and vigor as protecting one of his own. He could destroy the enemy and at the same time breathe life into his family with his love, patience, and a gentle spirit. I watched Alex when Alexander was born. Never have I seen a man so full of pride, hope, and validation that his service to our country was worth risking his life in order to protect his son or sons and daughters across our country. I saw the softer side in him, and I saw him bring out the softer side of his one true love. The past five years since bringing him into Atropos has been nothing short of remarkable. What he has taught each of us we will carry on until we join him in the afterlife. Despite never serving together, I know fellow Atropos men will welcome him with a warrior's hooah! Today we send you off, Alex, to meet your Atropos brothers. HOOAH!"

David, Alexander, Donovan, and the rest of the Atropos team raise their rifles high to the sky, preparing the rounds to travel alongside Alex's spirit. Together they fire. Norma flinches and recalls the sound of the round that took Alex away from her.

David removes the flag from Alex's coffin, then folds it with the Atropos men. After the last fold, then tuck, his hands extend, regretfully presenting it to Norma. "You are not alone. Let us be here for you. Let me help you through this. You don't always have to be so damn strong."

Norma takes it from David while refusing to peel her eyes from the coffin where she envisions Alex lying. Every fiber of her deadening being wants to be with him. She hands it right to Alex's legacy. Alexander accepts it with pride. His appearance is very much different than Norma's but still somberly to say the least. His father was his best friend. Alexander too has a hole in his heart that bleeds with sorrow.

David pulls his phone out to follow Atropos tradition. A tradition Norma conceived and insisted at the gravesite of fallen Atropos. It was to honor them. This time it was Alex's turn to fly high with his favorite flight song that he newly insisted on playing. The song replayed each time flying high, preparing for the deadly journey ahead.

The typewriter and accordion begin to play, then, "Whoa, come with now," belts from the speaker. One by one, as the music plays, they pass Alex's coffin, placing spent casings in a line on top. One by one, they whisper the Atropos truism to Alex, "*Donec mors nos separaverit*" (Until death separates us).

It has been three months since Norma returned to the home her and Alex had built together. It is here where they raised Alexander and spent many nights walking along the sandy beach at Cape Hatteras, talking and taking in the moist salty air. Witty tales about the antics of Alexander and Kratos, the family wolf hybrid, would be told by the dark moonlight while seagulls quietly slept on sandbars after a day of swimming in the air. The only things off-limits on this beach were stories of work and the darkness that surrounded them. Too often words were silenced by the ocean singing operatic sounds from waves crashing only to return like a creased roll of cyan-blue. It was like caviar for their souls.

Imprints of her feet sink deeply into the sand as her tears no longer recede with the waves, pulling back into the ocean. The wells of her eyes have been dry for months. Norma sits quietly as the white truffles wash up around her. It is winter cold but she is no longer able to feel. Donovan and David have been overseeing Alexander and Atropos as she fights the toughest battle since the time Alexander was born. Norma has never felt this before. Sure she has felt loss, just nothing that could cripple her. She dismisses Alexander, David, and Donovan's suggestion that she get grief counseling. Her thinking is that all her soul needs is its mate. Until then, nothing of this Earth could help her.

As her toes weave between the pebbly grains, Norma thinks of Kratos, which died a couple years back. Her eyes close to see him clearly running with Alex on the beach, then later lying on the dojo mats as Norma and Alex trained. Norma had always proved to be a fine trainer on deadly missions.

She taught Atropos to make the enemy die for their cause as they live for theirs. Always careful that one turn of the back could prove fatal. She then hears Alexander's words that age has somehow lessened her. That now in her mid-forties, however capable, the bullet pierces just slightly off target. It was not long after Alex's death that guilt crept in like a thief, stealing her ability to sleep, eat, and feel a desire to live. *Why didn't he check?* she wonders. *Why didn't I check?* never leaves her thoughts.

Her dark thoughts are lost in the deep blue sea as the sound of crunching sand comes closer. Norma looks back to see David approaching. His smile is as warming as the rising sun that's beginning to peak over billowy clouds. Except for Norma, darkness remains. Light left her three months ago and has yet returned. David refuses to listen to her request to be alone. He has dropped in no less than once a day to rid the fear of Norma joining Alex as she so desperately desires. It is well known that if not for Alexander, her story could end.

David removes his shoes and sits next to her. Her skin is as rigid as the wintry sand and cold as the icy water. He unzips his jacket, slips it off, then drapes it over Norma's numbed body. He wraps her, keeping only silence between them. Her eyes never break from the turbulent and unforgiving waves. She draws on its lonely mystical power. Soon her blue lips soften as promising words warm the air. Norma looks to him. "I need to get out of here," she says. Finally words David has longed to hear.

"Have you been out here all night?" he asks.

"Yes," she says. Norma peels away David's jacket and hands it back to him. It is no longer needed. She stands and begins to walk. "Hire someone to come in to remove his things and store them away from the house. Tell Alexander only where he can find his father's keepings." Until now their house has been untouched, frozen in time as she waited for Alex to return. She feels what it must have been like for Alex when he was facing another lonely sunrise, then sunset without her. How the idea of her lost presence was consuming. Unlike Alex, scented pillows or sprits chilling in the freezer will not have her chasing ghosts. If spring is to come, she must accept the darkness with hope to see the brightness of another day.

"Did you fly here alone?" she asks. Norma nears the house, looking to the helipad.

"Yes," David says. "Alexander stayed home." David stops to put his shoes back on before stepping onto the frosty pavers. As each lace threads then fills a hole, he fills in the gap since Norma last saw Alexander. "Without waiver, he has led Atropos. He is stronger, focused. Alex would be proud. You would be proud, Norma." He calls for her attention. She looks to him as a sense of pride breaches the deadness. "His bravery, his force is you." For the first time since that abandoned industrial building, Norma smiles. "Norma," David calls out. "You can't blame yourself."

"Can't I?" she says.

CHAPTER 8

Alexander walks toward Mr. Henry, forging a smile to ease Mr. Henry's concern for him. Mr. Henry, learning of Alexander's loss, has been extra attentive to him. Alexander sees him. He sees Mr. Henry for all the wonder, all the benevolence that he is. Alexander dreads the day he returns home from a mission only to learn that Mr. Henry has left the Penn Quarter of Washington, DC. That he will no longer be there to lie about a wound, a darkened eye, or broken bone being caused by a death match in some bull ring or, dare we say, a bullshit story to explain his battered appearance. Mr. Henry often urges Alexander to give up such reckless hobbies. Today, Alexander is sweaty and panting misty clouds out into the frigid winter air as he catches his breath from a long run.

"How are you, Mr. Henry?"

"Oh, I can't complain, Mr. Alexander. Can I get you anything today, sir? How was your run?"

Alexander pats him on the back. "All the years I've been here and you still won't stop calling me sir. People need to call you 'sir.' Mr. Henry, you could be my grandfather." Alexander feels that to be true. Although of different blood, their hearts are similar. They share the same fondness for each other. Over the past few months Alexander notices that frailness has taken over Mr. Henry's appearance. His skin has sunken deeper, and squiggly lines cover his cheeks and surround his broadening nose. Short silvery wisps are all that remain in once cheerful curls. His spine aches to stand upright.

"Have you seen Nyx today?" Alexander asks.

Mr. Henry's lips thin as big white choppers appear with a chuckle. He has watched the overpowering chemistry grow stronger between Alexander and Nyx over the last couple of months as Nyx has comforted Alexander—the slight touch of the small of her back as Alexander follows closely beside her as she walks through doors, the way Alexander and Nyx gaze into each other's eyes as they stop to say hi to Mr. Henry before entering the building. Even if decades upon decades have passed, Mr. Henry recognizes that look. The same look he gave his wife the day he stomped the glass, then hearing "Mazel Tov!" Delight for Alexander shows with Mr. Henry's joyous smile.

"No, Mr. Alexander. I think she's already left for work." Mr. Henry can sense Alexander's regret that getting lost in his run caused him to miss her. "I'm sure you two lovebirds will see each other tonight," he says. Alexander hopes that to be true. That a call will not keep them apart, then the time it will take a vial of THR to do its magic so as not to have to explain the damage he has endured from a recent mission. To Nyx, his bullshit stories seem to stink more and more. Now, THR and a night at The World Renaissance Hotel are essential before grooming for a date that has been planned.

"Very well," Alexander says. He takes a second to really measure Mr. Henry. "Do you mind if I pry?" he asks. "I don't want to overstep boundaries here, but I keep wondering…" Alexander pauses for the right words. "Why are you here? Why, after all the years of subways, bus rides, walking to tend to the needs of others, aren't you home tending to your need to relax and enjoy your family? I know I keep asking you but why? Go spend time with your wife, take a vacation, hell… spend time with those beautiful grandbabies and great-grandbabies," Alexander persists.

"That would be nice," Mr. Henry says. An exhausting sigh, then: "Maybe one day. Maybe one day I'll win the lottery." Worry riddles Mr. Henry's face and, for the first time since mourning blinded him, Alexander's cloudy eyes clear and he notices. Alexander continues to question until Mr. Henry's trained compliancy forces him to answer. Mr. Henry's heart weeps with the story that two months ago his five-year-old granddaughter was diagnosed with nephroblastoma, Wilms' tumor, a rare kidney cancer. His daughter had been abandoned by her husband and moved in with him working three jobs to afford the medical costs. That despair has depleted his pension and hope was diminishing his savings. Alexander can hear no more.

"Why didn't you tell me?" he yells.

"I'm not here to trouble you, Mr. Alexander. We will be aight," he says, as if to comfort Alexander. That worry was wasted and that somehow hope would heal and save his granddaughter.

The world seemed bitter to Alexander at times, especially this time. He feels helpless understanding his place and contemplates how he could help. Alexander once again pats Mr. Henry on his curving back and begins to walk off, only to stop to look back in bewilderment. He must do something, he is certain, but that will take time to reveal itself.

CHAPTER 9

Alexander can see the sunset on the horizon from his penthouse windows. The bold reds and brilliant, rich oranges are fleeting and beginning to fade to darkness. His thoughts of Mr. Henry have weighed heavily on him for the past few hours, until Nyx enters his mind. His shoulders feel lighter and he smiles. An expected tap on his door has him rushing to open it. As the door opens wider her bright hazel eyes shine through. These are the lips he has been hungering to taste all day. Quickly Alexander grabs Nyx and pulls her in, slamming the door shut. He softly grabs behind her neck, passionately tasting her glossy, berry lips. The straps that are dangling on her fingers slip, dropping her heels to the floor. Her feet have been aching from a day at the studio, so she opted to be barefoot for the elevator ride up. Nyx rises on her tiptoes to wrap her arms around him. The heat from their bodies pressing tightly together rids February's shivering air. "I have missed you," she softly whispers in his ear as her warming nipples perk hard, aroused.

Alexander slowly guides her to the couch, then stops. His patient hands gradually remove layer by layer, tossing each to the ground until all that remains standing is her perfect breast, smooth stomach, and carved, toned muscles that decorate her body like a beautiful swan with wings spanning, ready. His skin beads with lusting sweat as he kisses down her soft, scented flesh. Her fingers get lost in his hair as he bends lower and lower, gently caressing her body with his lips and tongue. He stops where he is sure her wings will span wider and she will take flight. His tongue moves in deeper, tasting all of her. Nyx's eyes close, legs tighten, her head arches back, when an explosive rush comes over her quivering body. Her wet vagina pulsates with each pounding heartbeat, ready to wrap and absorb his pleasuring essence. Alexander rises quickly, unzipping his pants unveiling his hard, swollen excitement. He slowly lowers her to the couch. Her legs wrap him as he gently slides into her, filling her deep.

She grabs Alexander, then releases to grab firmly a pillow that has been lying next to her head. The pillow muffles her moans. Alexander takes the pillow from her face to look deep into her eyes. He can feel her warmth wrapped around him as his heart pumps hard with each grinding motion. He begins to move slow and smooth as his heart guides his hips, craving for this to last. His lips softly nibble on her neck where he can feel her throbbing pleasure. Satisfying moans roam freely while hot breath runs down her neck. He can feel her fingers bury deep into his back, pulling him in closer to feel more. She closed on it as tight as she could—not wanting to let go. He returns his eyes to hers—losing himself within her. Their lips press together, then their tongues waltz.

It is an hour before their entwined bodies come, then fall apart. Alexander released his thick relish, racing to be first while his legs are lastly weakened. They are spent. Nyx can feel Alexander's heart pound, then slowly calm. He softly kisses her, then falls to her side, breathless, as their bodies glisten.

Nyx turns her head to look at Alexander. Her expression is vulnerable. For the first time: "I love you," she says.

Alexander frightens. His soul wants to shout out *I love you,* but his head screams for a sensible distance. She could never be a part of his world, he has been warned. Zen soon turns ruffled at the thought that his impulsive craving may leave an undesirable outcome. The unrequited love painfully stings Nyx.

"I have to go," she says. Nyx abruptly rises, then dresses, preparing to leave. Alexander pulls his pants up, then zips, leaving the top button open. The sweat is still dripping between the ripples of his stomach. His hand reaches for hers, but she shies away.

"Don't go," he says. He reaches again this time she allows her petite hand to swallow into his. "You know how I feel about you. Nyx, look at me." Alexander takes her chin in his hand and lifts her eyes to look at him. "You know how I feel. There is so much you don't know and I can't tell you."

"Can't or won't?" she asks, moving her face away from him. "You never let me sleep here or come to my place. You reflect when I show interest about your work…We have been dating for almost three months… Why can't I meet your mother?"

That loaded question shot straight to Alexander's core. He sees Norma's disapproving face. This relationship is forbidden. It has been an unbreakable vow since the beginning—except for once. He wants to give to her freely but hand-holding down the sidewalks within Washington, DC, could be fatal to Nyx. She could become a moving pawn on a chess match that could prove direr than the last time Alexander disobediently played the game. The chess game that ultimately led him to Atropos.

"Give me time," he says. His fingers brush her auburn hair away from her face to see her sodden eyes. He wants desperately to say the words she craves to hear. But again, he feels: *What is the point?* "I'll be gone for a couple of days. Can I see you when I get back?"

Nyx turns to walk away heading for the door as Alexander follows closely. In one hand her heels dangle by the straps and in the other the knob stops turning. She spins around dropping her shoes and wraps her arms around Alexander pulling him in close to her. Her head tenderly rests on his firm bare chest. "You don't have to tell me, I know you love me. What I felt for you the day we met is not like any other. I know you feel the same way. This can't be wrong Alexander."

He responds holding her tightly against him, giving her assurance that her love is indeed requited.

An unexpected knock taps at the door startling Alexander and Nyx. Alexander reaches over Nyx and hesitantly opens the door to see what he fears most looking back at him. "Mom," he says. Norma stands in the doorway reluctant to come in as her expressionless face speaks loudly to Alexander. He commits to seizing the moment he did well to avoid. He fearlessly steps back, then gives Nyx what her heart desires. "Mom, this is Nyx," he says, motioning for Norma to enter.

Norma steps past Nyx with authority and without delay begins the profile. She notes that Nyx must be innocent to their world and who Norma really is by Nyx's calm manner. That by the calluses on her feet and feminine muscles, ribbons have wrapped her ankles since she was old enough to stand in first position. She must be from nobility or prime, scoring the leading role to be living in these lavish condos and so well-tailored at her young age. Norma would judge rightly that Nyx is just a year older than Alexander. She is twenty-seven. Nyx is smart, educated, confident, and beautiful but not in a way that she knows it. Norma can see what Alexander sees, yet she stands, averring this must not continue. He must stay faithful to Atropos.

"It is very nice to meet you," Norma says, offering Nyx an affable hand. "Is your name an accident or were your parents into Greek mythology?" Amused and curious, Alexander is unsure why, of all times, Norma cares.

Nyx bashfully responds, sensing a compelling presence before her. "My father was a big Greek mythology nerd. They always said I was named right. As a baby I refused sleep and stayed up all night. That at 'terrible two' they were beginning to believe I was in fact the daughter of chaos." Norma was intimidating, and Nyx felt it no less as Norma stood unresponsive, hearing Nyx's childhood tale. Nyx cannot discern if it is a grief-stricken Norma that has made her so closed off, or is it just Norma's chilling personality. "I'm sorry about Alex," she says.

Norma removes her form fitting jacket that shows years of sculpted muscles, then drapes it over her arm. The lines in her forearm and bicep flinch. Norma is poised, polished, and statuesque, with mesmerizing beauty. A lofty smile forms on her face. “Thank you,” she says, walking deeper into Alexander’s living room. “I will give you two a moment to say goodbye.”

Nyx reaches to kiss Alexander. Alexander passes her lips and kisses her on the cheek. “I will call you when I get back from my trip.” His hand touches the small of her back and guides her out the door. Nyx looks back now, not wanting to go. Her lips mouth the words *I love you*. Alexander smiles and boldly says in Latin, “*Me quoque*” (Me too) loud enough for Norma to hear. He shuts the door, then returns to his reality.

“We need to talk,” Norma says.

CHAPTER 10

In uncertain times prevailing tradition offers a sense of normalcy, a sense of purpose, a sense of security.

"Listen up," shouts from the podium. It is a sound heard since the beginning. The beginning when a young eighteen-year-old Norma was appointed leader, then naming the newly formed team Atropos, after the Greek goddess of fate. Some that have long been gone, some that were more recent lost, and some remaining have heard Donovan silence the room with those two words. Alexander and David take the two front row seats while others sit behind them. Xavier pushes on Alexander's back. Alexander turns around as Xavier begins to sing, "If I was a Nyx girl. Nanananana..."

"Shut up, dumbass," Alexander laughs, and then turns to David. "Did you tell him?" Alexander asks. David shakes his head no, then shrugs his shoulders with a pretty sound theory crossing his mind. Alexander sits pondering his own assumption. His cell phone buzzes from his pocket. Alexander swipes to open the message from Nyx. He reads: *This can't be wrong.*

Light footsteps can be heard walking up the aisle as silence takes over row upon row until the room is completely still. Norma reaches the front, then turns to stand next to Donovan at the wood podium with the original A still branded in the middle. Donovan nods his head to her as if to bow while using his cane for balance. He grins. Excitement to have her back fills the room with renewed energy. Norma looks to Atropos with boldness. She is not broken. She stands, audacious, and thirsty for revenge.

Alexander, David, and Xavier immediately spring to their feet, then the remaining Atropos men stand. Hands spiritedly clap as "Hooah" sounds off. Their true leader has once again returned. A little light peeks through the darkness as she witnesses them proudly welcome her back. Norma raises her hands to motion them to sit and be quiet as she begins to speak.

"I want to thank you all for the support that you have shown me, as we all go through this most difficult time. It has not gone unnoticed that not only did I lose a husband and Alexander lost a father, but you men lost a brother. When we accepted this life we knew it would come with a price. A price that we all are willing to pay for the good of our country, and the people we vowed to protect, even when they don't see or can feel the atrocities that surround us. Borders we often cross in order to right the wrongs, to keep the boogeyman a figment of a child's imagination. Still, there are times when that cost will deplete the soul as it has mine. It leaves you wondering if the price was too much. But then you see your young son running through your memories, becoming a man." Norma glances over to Alexander and smiles. "And you realize who else is so ready to feel the sharp cut that we so diligently train to accept. We are! We are valiant, we are Atropos! We will sacrifice and do what others shall never see, never feel, never accept."

Xavier jumps to his feet. "Hooah," he yells. "Fuck yeah! Atropos!"

Ten men stand planting their feet, chanting "Atropos." Alexander sees his mother wink and cannot help but wonder if there is more than inspiration working here. Were the other nine men meant to reinforce what he already knows? Nyx enters his mind. The feeling of loss overcomes him. He knows what he must do. Douse the chemistry before it ignites a life of its own and causes him failure.

"Okay, everyone take a seat. We have a lot to go over before you all head out tonight," Donovan says. He limps with a cane that relieves the duty of his right leg. Agency-issued TRH healed the wounds but the missing bone remains in that abandoned building. Norma leaves the podium and pulls a folding chair to sit next to David. She looks attentively at the screen as Donovan flashes through pictures of Middle Eastern men never seen before, coordinates as to where boots will drop in sand, and briefs on the mission ahead. A newly constructed, unoccupied airport pops up on the screen. Donovan points, using the cursor.

"You will land at this international airport near Duhok, Iraq. Don't worry; it is not being used. Funding dried up, and the construction company went belly up. Until a bid is won to complete it, we have it to use, undetected. An agency keeper will be waiting to take you a few miles to the far top side of the mountain that borders Duhok. From there you will trek down to spy on this hotel on the edge of town." Donovan clicks the airport away, then clicks a picture of a hotel to the front of the screen—the cursor points. "Those men I just showed you have been seen entering and leaving this hotel and were previously spotted with Chris Logan. It's what leads us to here. It is believed, by the intel received, that the one who ordered the hit on Alexander, then at Big Lou's, hides out at this hotel. We still don't know who he is, but we do know that these are his henchmen."

There are more grains needed to form a solid-rock conclusion. Donovan stalls on the last group of pictures and looks to Norma. He waits for her response. Norma nods, then Donovan clicks. It is Chris Logan with a big red X over his face. David, Xavier, and the Atropos men look to Alexander, then Norma, waiting for their reaction. Norma sits looking at the screen. She is no longer daunted by his image. The only ghost allowed to enter her dreams at night is Alex. Alexander looks to his solid mother. Donovan continues with additional red X's back to back. They were the faces at Big Lou's Diner and the gunman who Norma took out at the Lincoln Memorial. Donovan continues.

"Men, this it is to be uncomplicated." He guarantees all will return, and no one will die. Donovan goes on to say that it is still unclear how deep this pocket is and the lengths to which they operate. They know of a connection to Chris Logan and the Lesser Caucasus, and of a connection to Chris Logan and the men they see in the pictures, yet they still don't know who the puppet master is. It is the agency's hope that Atropos will return from the mountain in Duhok with enough strings to tie this in order. It is Norma's hope to finally quench her thirst for revenge on the one who ordered their capture.

CHAPTER 11

Duhok, Iraqi Kurdistan Region.

In a line Alexander's hand motions to move out. Atropos, with Raiden on point, treks down the broad, wet, sandy plains of the Zawa mountain of Duhok. The one-inch-by-one-inch eyepiece attached to their caps drops down over their eyes to overlay a map through high-definition field vision, offering target information. It's wirelessly connected to Alexander's watch and thermal sites mounted on their rifles. As they move forward its vivid images record everything from far into the nestled city. Terrain, people, vehicles are all taken into the third eye that streams live for Donovan and Norma to receive a visual as to what is before them. Headsets over hats allow them to speak freely through private channels to each other and to Norma and Donovan. Back at the agency in Donovan's office in Washington, DC, Norma can see even a rat scuttling out from the hotel on multiple screens, leaving no angle overlooked.

Xavier grabs Alexander and pulls him in close. His tongue and lips flicker at Alexander's eyepiece, seeming to lick and kiss it. Through jumbling lines Xavier hears Norma loud and clear: "Stop fucking around. If anything goes wrong, I will kill you myself."

The rain begins to fall sideways, cloaking their position. It is not quite as cold as winter in Washington, DC, but a breezy fifty-seven degrees and a wet ensemble dampens the Atropos spirit. The stealth helicopter had just left them on the far side of the mountain and the men already anticipate their rendezvous time.

"Can you think of a better way to spend eight hours at the office?" Lander says. Just below his hat and tan skull cap, blond strands that are peeking out have darkened from the rain as bright red, blotchy patches cover his pale face.

Heavy showers even quiet the Iraq Babbler's high-pitched *pi-pi-pi-pi* that welcomes the early-morning dawn. They are beginning to believe they are the only creatures stirring in this early morning downpour. As they creep, Xavier spies something moving alongside the Tigris River—a ravening grey wolf stalking its prey. *How appropriate,* he thinks. Norma sees through Xavier's eye and sighs as the wolf makes his morning kill. Soon the hungry wolf shifts into Kratos, eating breakfast at his bowl.

Alexander barks orders to spread out and hunker down. They are as far as they need to be. The eyepieces will travel the rest of the way for the intel needed. Atropos sits and waits while the shower continues. They take turns as eyelids become heavy and occasionally steal a moment to close while the third eye on their hat remains wide open. These lenses are indifferent to the eight-hour time difference. Lucky for Alexander, when it is his turn to rest, a playback from his day drifting cannot stream to Washington, DC. As Atropos waits for the men in the pictures to show their faces, another face appears to Alexander. He can hear her whisper *I love you* as her vulnerable eyes stare deep into his. He snaps awake. *Mom is right,* he thinks. *It has to end. 'Emotions can distract and destroy you,'* he hears Norma say. That seems to him to be shittier than the soupy goat pellets nearby. He looks to David, wanting guidance. *With all the years passed, how has David managed his obvious love for Norma?* Alexander wonders. Alexander moves to David's side and sits uncomfortably on the wet rock fragments with the idea of what he is about to ask. "Mute your mic and don't look at me. You know Mom could read what I am about to say." Keeping eyes forward, Alexander takes David somewhere more precarious. "Be honest with me. Have you always been in love with my mother?" He waits for the answer he does not want to hear. The sharpness of the rock fragments suddenly seem to be less agonizing.

David begins to squirm, uneasy yet with the death of Alex; he feels no need to hide in safe shadows. "Yes," he says. A slight grin takes over his face. "Your mother and I had a moment; until she met your father. Then it was over. She loved your father, and I had to sit on the sidelines watching as he got to live the life I wanted. But if that was all I was fated for, I accepted it gladly. Just as long as I still shared some part of her life. Remember, we met when we were both eighteen." David gets lost in distant memories.

Alexander begins to see David differently. Not good, not bad, just different. He felt the probable pain if forced to watch

Nyx move away from him. "How do you live in our world with that? Is Mom right? Does emotion distract and destroy you?"

"I don't know son. After seeing what your mom went through losing your dad…What I felt when I thought she was dead…Maybe she is right. Still you have to remember your mom left Atropos when you were born and other than training together my time was limited with her. I spent twenty years trying to forget the love I have for her."

"Is it possible to live in our world and be with someone that isn't?"

"Your dad did for a long time. He wasn't Atropos at the beginning. Rick felt him to be incapable."

Alexander shuns that notion. His father was the bravest he was certain. "But he was black ops. What if the other person is just an ordinary person?"

"I am assuming this is about Nyx?"

"Mom dropped in while she was there. They met."

David laughs. "Oh lord. Is Nyx still alive?"

"Seriously. That motivational speech was more for me and less to remind you all of our vow. I can't get this woman out of my head. I was determined to break it off with her but I can't. I don't want to. After Dad died, you all thought I was focused, strong, but inside I taunted the reaper. Now…she's made me cautious."

David can see himself in Alexander as he spoke the last sentence. He sighs. "You have fallen in love with her… Well kiddo…this isn't going to get solved here on this mountain that I am sure of. When we get back, let me feel your mother out."

Alexander spots an Infiniti sedan pulling up to the International hotel that was in their briefing. A Middle Eastern man walks out from the front lobby door and stops near the sedan door looking ready to get in. This is the car they were briefed on—Silver, 2012, G25. The car door swings open and a younger man, if you had to guess Alexander's age, steps out. "Holy shit," Alexander says. "Look at him." Binoculars zoom in a little closer. "He is a younger version of the leader we killed in the Lesser Caucasus. Look!" This man was not in Donovan's lineup shown earlier. "Who is that?"

As the man gets out he reaches back to retrieve something. Alexander and David look to the other men, ensuring this is getting captured from every angle. A little girl, five maybe six, is forced out of the car. She is not Middle Eastern as the two men are. She looks to be of Spanish descent. They escort her into the hotel just as two more young girls and a boy ranging in age from seven to thirteen are escorted out and into the sedan. The unexpected footage streams confusion back to Norma and Donovan.

"What is this place?" Alexander asks. Each Atropos man shares the same puzzling expression, waiting for faces that have been marked to complete the picture. The intel needed was thought to uncover a terrorist cell operating within this hotel. Key players tied to all the ones they took out before that had plotted for attacks on American soil. *Who are these children?* haunts the Atropos team.

Hours of heavy rain pound leaving the men with wrinkly, pruney fingers and glabrous skin sensitive to the cold trigger. They are eager for the flight home and dry clothes. This is not a preferred mission; it's one they feel is more suitable for a different type of agency team. Collecting intel is not something any of these men feel is time or Atropos resources well spent. To them it would be the equivalent to using the AH-60 stealth helicopter that's parked just a few miles away at the airport construction site as an air taxi for bloated politicians.

Xavier walks, crouching toward Alexander and David. "I don't think we're going to get what we came for. The chopper will be here in thirty. Can we please go home now? My ass is waterlogged, and I think Mother Nature used her teeth and frostbit my dick. I can't feel it anymore, it's numb. I think it's shriveled up to a man-gina now."

"Makes sense," Alexander says. He playfully punches Xavier on his brawny chest and adds, "We always knew you were a pussy." Xavier mocks Alexander, then obnoxiously chuckles foolish sounds.

"What would you know about pussy?" Xavier laughs. "Oh yeah, if I was a Nyx girl, nanananana." He looks into the third eye where he believes Norma is watching and pumps his hips back and forth, simulating sex. Alexander pushes Xavier away. He is more than aware his mother and Donovan are watching, along with David and the Atropos men.

"Xavier, really! Who fucking damaged you?" Alexander says.

The men swap playful punches as Atropos comes together. Lander, shortest of the group, is five foot eight, stocky build but can easily hold his own against Xavier. Some even say he has resumed Dorian's steps with slinging continuous stabs at Xavier. "Man-child," he calls Xavier. The men laugh.

"Fuck you, shorty," Xavier says. Lander is half of Xavier's forty-five years and rightfully the one you would expect to engage in such juvenile silliness. Xavier looks down the line of young faces. "I don't know what any of you all are laughing at. The only pussy you shit-faces have ever been pressed against was your momma's when she was grunting to shit your ugly asses out. You're a bunch of cock snots." The windy rain drowns the hearty laughs from echoing down the mountain. The banter is thick as the cold mist. Still, Xavier is the center of Atropos lore, spinning tales of enemies losing ears, enemies exploding as he runs to shower in his glory, and even a rumor that he once bared his butt and pressed it against dead enemy lips, saying, 'Here, you wanted to kiss my ass goodbye, kiss it.' but yet he has never forgotten a single Atropos birthday. Some speculate he is deeper than the frivolity he portrays.

"Enough," David says.

"All right, guys, let's get ready to move out," Alexander commands.

As the men begin to turn and trail up the mountain to board the idling helicopter, Raiden catches sight of the same Infiniti sedan pulling up to the hotel. It had left only forty minutes ago—maybe forty-five, tops. The same Middle Eastern man exits the car, then enters the hotel.

The lenses zoom in identifying the doppelganger of the dead leader in the Lesser Caucasus. Alexander responds into his mic agreeing *it has to be* as the team assumes he is confirming with Norma that this man must be the dead terrorist leader's son. Being in the family business seems as ubiquitous here as it is in Atropos. The similarities are eerie. In no more than a mere minute he is seen leaving the hotel with a little girl tightly gripped in his hand. She is white, blond, and no more than seven. By the clothes she is wearing, one would say she is European or American. "What is this place?" Alexander says.

"Let's go find out," Xavier says. He fidgets and is cocked, ready for action.

"We can't compromise us," David says. His eyes say differently as do the remaining eyes firmly pressing to zoom in even closer. Atropos men watch and record. As the man and little girl near the car, the door opens. The little girl yanks pulling away when she spots a man with a puppy nearby. She runs. The furry, tail wagging pup jumps wildly, excitably ready to play with her. The owner smiles as the little girl bends to pet and cuddle him as she looks up to the man holding the leash. She appears to be scared and hesitant to talk. The leader's doppelganger storms near them outwardly angry. He snatches the little girl up and regains control of her. A gun is taken from his waist. He aims down and shoots the puppy dead.

"What the fuck did we just see?" Milo questions.

"What the fuck," echoes as Alexander, David, Lander, Kosmo, Stefen, Raiden, Vali, Nick, and Xavier face looking at each other for affirmation that their eyes are not deceiving them. Xavier bull rushes past everyone on a path down to where the dead puppy lays.

"Get back here," Alexander yells. He sternly calls Xavier again, then Xavier slowly returns, keeping his sight down that mountain. "This is not the time. We have no idea what just happened and we don't need to shoot off half-cocked. We haven't been given the order for this."

"Stand down," Norma's voice sternly orders through the headset.

"That's bullshit," Xavier says, then calms his notions to realize even if at full speed, even by the stealth helicopter that awaits them, by the time they reached either the top or the bottom it would be too late. The car would be gone as to the little girl in it.

CHAPTER 12

As Norma waits for the Atropos team to arrive at The World Renaissance Hotel for keepers to tend to their needs, then debriefing, she takes the time to study all the pieces that have been collected. So much is unclear, so much does not fit. Now with new players and children that look not to belong in this shift shaping puzzle more time is crucial. Donovan enters his office and stands next to Norma as she sits in his wingback chair replaying and studying each video, picture, and face. She creates corners with old faces in hopes the new images will fit inside nicely. Since returning to the agency this is where she leads, as she has not been to the office that she and Alex once shared. The scent of Alex trapped behind those doors would be too much to bear. To be exact, she has yet to return to her home in Hatteras. Here and The World Renaissance Hotel is where she will stay. At least for now.

"Anything?" Donovan asks.

"Not yet," she says. Her fingers brush through her soft raven hair, and she softly bites her lower lip. Frustration riddles her face. Her head bends left, then right, then *crack, crack, crack* sounds from her neck.

"Keep scowling like that and you're going to see a wrinkle soon," Donovan says, attempting to lighten her grave look.

His comment passes through her ears and lands flat, unnoticed. "Who were those kids?" she asks, irritated that with all that is in front of her, the answer still eludes her.

"That, I do not know," Donovan says.

Norma rises from the chair, allowing Donovan to take his seat. "I need to run and clear my head." She goes to the gym bag resting in the chair in front of Donovan's desk and opens it. She unbuttons, then removes her shirt. Donovan sits in front of the screens, taking his turn to fit the pieces (impervious to Norma) together. Atropos men seeing Norma strip down to a sports bra and tight shorts was not unusual. Besides, thanks to Chris Logan, it is not like Donovan hasn't already seen her naked body. Donovan looks to Norma with a thought sparking but notices the long scar down her back. From the manuscript left at Mackenzie's apartment, he remembers the story that vividly described the day her father left his mark. The day her mother died inside of her, and the day Mackenzie made her capable of enduring Chris Logan's madness. The desire to pick up where he was stopped inside of that abandoned warehouse overcomes him. "Norma," he calls. She turns around as she slides a running jacket on. "I should have stopped him," Donovan says.

"Who?" she asks as she pulls up tight leggings, then laces her racing shoes.

"Your father," Donovan says.

"Don't, Donovan!" Norma stops him as she glances over, then continues to prepare for her run. Her cell phone rings. Anticipating Alexander's call, Norma quickly takes it from Donovan's desk and answers it. By her expression, this is not the voice she anticipated to hear. "Yes," she says. She looks to Donovan with bothered eyes. "What can I do for you mother?" she adds. After another yes, then the location at her favored coffee shop to meet, Norma hangs up. "I don't have time for this," Norma says.

"What does she want?" Donovan asks.

"She heard of Alex's death and wants to see if I am okay. She is in town. A little late, wouldn't you say?" Norma places her folded clothes into the bag and reaches for the door. She looks back to Donovan. "I have no idea why I agreed to this. She shut that door many years ago. Why she wants to reopen it now is not my concern."

"Call her back and tell her you can't make it," Donovan says.

"It's fine. I had planned on running for coffee anyway. Besides she said she had something for Alexander. I'd rather intercept before she calls on him next. He has had *enough* distractions lately."

Norma slows her feet as she nears the coffee bar on H Street NE. As her heated breath puffs clouds into the wintry air, she can see Eva sitting at the bar near the glass window, waiting patiently. She stops just outside of Eva's view just for a moment to study her mother. She is even frailer than the last time she saw her—at her father's funeral over five years ago. The winter jacket is zipped tightly over her hunching, plump body, and her stockings appear as loose as the crinkly skin they cover. Well into her seventh decade of life, Eva looks to be closer to her ninth. Through the window Norma can see pink puffy sacs below her mother's withered and bitter eyes and thin silvery bangs peeking out from under a pink crocheted beanie. *What is she looking at?* Norma wonders as she notices Eva staring dismally at a picture. *Let's get this over with,* Norma thinks.

Norma opens the glass door, then passes the barista to walk toward the window bar. Eva looks up and perks as bold as the coffee nearby when Norma nears. "Hi, honey," she says. Norma's flesh shivers with goose bumps as Eva rises to embrace her. With hesitation, Norma accepts her.

"What can I do for you, Mother?" Norma asks.

"I just wanted to check on you after I'd heard about Alex's death. How ya doing, hun? Was he ill for long?" Norma looks forward to the opportunity to thank her brother Willie. Seeing that Alexander and Willie are the only known surviving relatives to Norma, it was not a hard deduction as to who delivered the devastating news to Eva.

"No, Mother, it was a training accident...but we are fine. Alexander and I will be fine. What is it that you wanted me to give Alexander?" Norma nudges Eva to follow her to the counter, where the city's best barista waits to fill their order. "This place has the best coffee and blackberry lavender scone in town. Can I buy you one?"

Intimidated by the menu of espressos, lattes, pour-overs and just about any coffee drink you can imagine, Eva fumbles, copying Norma's order. As they wait for beans to grind, then brew, Eva admires the beautiful tiles and wooden floors beneath the 1960s lighting. "This place is real fancy. It reminds me of Charleston," Eva says. Norma never knew her mother had traveled to Charleston. But then again, Norma doesn't know where her mother has been for the past forty years other than random sightings around her hometown when she was a kid.

Now Norma is beginning to brew and is eager to get back to the reason for her being here. "What would you like me to give Alexander?" she asks again.

They gather a few napkins, then take steaming aromatic coffee that's swirling into the air and warmed scones to the window bar and sit. Eva retrieves a picture from her pocket as Norma takes her first sip, then climbs onto the short wooden barstool. "I found this picture I had of your father when he was in the military. I thought Alexander would like to have it."

Norma rests the coffee cup on the bar, then takes the picture in hand. To say she was shocked, flabbergasted, taken back would be under citing her reaction right now. *Why in the hell would Alexander want a picture of his grandfather seeing he is the one that fired the shot that Norma couldn't, killing him?* Once care left and reasoning was no longer needed, Norma can't help but study the picture closer. Her father was very young, virile and full of life as were the men casually sitting around him in some secluded jungle area. Their rifles are loosely held or resting on a tree nearby. They are eating rations and drinking from canteens. Her eyes are drawn to one in particular. He is about the same age as her father. She can gather by long lanky legs bent that he is tall, skinny with a cigar dangling from his lips. She knows that face. It is Donovan.

His youthful image is now clear in her mind's eye. He is how she imagined. Norma studies her mother's empty smile as Eva enjoys a bite of her blueberry lavender scone, then returns to her father's youthful face. Was it here that the monster was made, or was it always a part of him? She ponders the dynamics of Eva and Mackenzie, then she and Alex, then Alexander and can't help but think: *If only it had been different.* She has accepted her stars, but Alexander. It was for this reason she left the agency. A different world was her hope for him. A different legacy. Pride is a given, that he is Atropos, but so, too, she is conflicting with a desire for a different path for him. Anger rushes for Rick. She thinks of Alexander and Nyx and what she may be denying him.

"You know, me and your father met soon after that picture was taken. I was living in DC when we were introduced by that guy there." Eva points to Donovan. "I was a file clerk at the Department of the Army when they both came in looking for a file on some soldier who had been recently discharged." Old files of memories, deeply tucked away, are fumbled through. "If I remember right, it wasn't long after that Willie was born." Eva lets out a naive, silly chuckle. "I remember being sick as dog with him. Still, not as bad as I was with you. I was constantly at the doctor's office getting a needle stuck in my belly from the day we found out I was pregnant. It wasn't a little needle, either. They were long. They said it was to make sure you were growing right." Eva's silly chuckle quickly turns to a scornful chortle. "Your daddy was no help, either. He was more concerned with you than the pain from those damn needles. All he ever did was scorn me like I was some damn child: 'Quit squirming! Dry your eyes.' All I heard on the car ride back was how I was weak, how I'd embarrass him."

Hearing how Donovan introduced them and the story of the long needles sparked Norma's interest. Her parents' relationship failures did not. She can remember the plates crashing and the night Eva walked out as if it were yesterday. Norma suddenly feels the need to speak to Donovan.

"Did that man ever come to visit us?" Norma asks pointing to Donovan.

"His name was Donnie. Yeah, pretty often," Eva says.

Norma searches her memories but cannot recall seeing Donovan prior to the agency.

"Well, that's until the day Donnie and your father got into a huge fight over something. I heard them yelling in the room, but the door was shut. Plus, they had turned the radio up so load I couldn't tell what they were saying. Donnie stormed out and I never saw him again...Your father sure knew how to piss people off," Eva says. She looks perplexed. "I don't know what ever happened to him."

Norma and Eva spend no more than the time it takes the steam from their coffee to stop wafting warm aromas up into the air before Norma politely excuses herself back to work. Eva saddens that her opportunity is leaving, then realizes that in reality her opportunity has been long gone. Norma looks back to her mother with the understanding that this may be the last time she sees her. Her days around the sun appear to be limited. Eva reaches for a farewell hug. Norma, again, reluctantly allows her embrace. "Take care, Mother," she says.

CHAPTER 13

Norma enters Donovan's office. He is sitting, studying the screen just as she had left him. The picture flops down onto his desk. Donovan retrieves it and smiles. "Oh my. Now that is a faded time that has almost been forgotten. Is that what Eva had for you? Wow," he says.

"Tell me about how you introduced them, Donnie. And I want to hear about needles while she was pregnant with me, and why in the hell am I am just learning about this?"

"I tried to tell you everything in the warehouse and before you left here to meet her. Hell, I tried to tell you five years ago when you stuck a gun in my back looking for answers." Donovan sighs, then takes his eyes off the picture to look at Norma.

"Was Alexander the first experiment? I had assumed it was Alexander that Rick first played God, trying to genetically alter Alexander with Alex's and David's DNA?" Norma begins to anger. She repeats, "Was he the first experiment? Or was I?"

"Neither," Donovan says. "Willie was. After Willie was born, he continued to show more traits of Eva than Mackenzie. He was fearful, timid, highly sensitive, and was slow and inept in completing fundamental tasks. Eva was chosen because she was timid and easily manipulated. Rick did not count on her genetics to override the stronger, more valiant DNA that he was injecting her with. You, on the other hand, were not conceived naturally then manufactured like Willie. Rick wanted to control Eva's eggs so he had ordered Mackenzie to give Eva fake birth control for when the time was right. When she came in for an OB-GYN appointment with Rick's private doctor, he transplanted the eggs taken from her previously, which had been fertilized with—" Donovan hesitates to tell her "—Mackenzie and Rick's sperm. When Mackenzie was instructed to move you all to Martinsburg, Rick knew that she would not intervene when the time came for Mackenzie to train or, if need be, to rid her and Willie. As you know, of course, that was after you were born and showing signs the transplant had been successful."

Norma's face drops and she gasps. Donovan's words has jumped from his lips and slapped the air from Norma's chest. Quickly the bombshell is replaced with an explosion. "Willie was a child! Who the fuck do you think you are? You treated us like animals trying to create a perfect specimen that you could exploit! You threw us to the wolves and had Willie discarded like he was damaged, worthless. Then you tried again with me!"

"I swear to you, Norma, I did not know. When I learned you were to be exterminated to gain access to Alexander, I could see clearly and knew that Rick's evil knew no bounds. It is why I intercepted you before the car exploded and hid you until you were healed. You are forgetting, when you awoke from the coma, you still did not trust me and left before I could explain all that I knew—"

"What the fuck did you expect?" Norma interrupts. "I realized in the hotel after the first mission that I was not meant to return. I knew it was Alexander that he wanted. Rick knew that if Alexander found that dairy he would seek answers from my father. He knew what Mackenzie would do him. He set us up! Why didn't you tell me?"

"Norma, I did not know! It was not even an hour before you found me in that alley, sticking a gun in my back for answers, trying to find Alexander; I sat in Rick's office and profiled the monster that he became. I went snooping for your file and only could get to a small part before Rick came in and interrupted me. Most of it was locked and encrypted in a file with his private doctor's name. You got to me before I could go back to try to crack into it even further back." Donovan recognizes that now is the time for all to come forth. "When we got back from the Lesser Caucasus Mountains, I called Rick's private doctor and informed him of Rick's death. I made it clear that you were the new director. You wanted your entire file. Everything Rick had been hiding… Norma, your mother, gave birth to super-fecundation twins…Two babies born with different fathers. The government's intracytoplasmic sperm injection program was in its infancy. I had him do a DNA test of your blood, and the blood samples on file for Rick and your father. You are a match with Mackenzie. Your stillborn twin was a match with Rick's DNA. Neither your mother nor father ever knew about your twin brother…about Rick's sperm being used. When it was time for delivery, they sedated her. She was forced to leave you with your father and to take Willie with her. She was just a pawn in Rick's game."

"It's been five years! Why hadn't you told me?" Norma asks.

"I tried. Once you confirmed David's DNA was not part of Alexander, you didn't care to know about you," Donovan says.

The smoky mirror dissipates, and Norma sees herself and Rick's agency clearly. She envisions Eva sitting at the coffee shop waiting for her to arrive. Norma sighs, seeing Eva as a timid, unsuspecting lamb.

"It is strange to understand her now. It is strange that for once we have something in common. It is sad that the man in that picture left her a shell of a woman as he did me," Norma says. She takes a moment to absorb all that has been said—a stillborn twin, Willie, Mackenzie, Eva, Rick, David, Alex, and Alexander. It is all too much to process right now. *Ridiculous,* she thinks. In a second, concern over Rick's sins leaves her. After all, it was her that sent him, with devil's breath, to eternal hell. So just like that, she shoos Donovan out of his seat, only to take it for herself.

"Move your crippled ass," she mumbles. Norma watches as Donovan strains to hoist himself up using the cane to balance him. "How are you doing with all that?" she asks, concerned that she sees the same frailness that she saw in her mother and that he, too, may be just another victim of this agency.

"Well. I sure as the hell won't be boarding any choppers or joining you guys in any fun anytime soon," he says.

"Your old ass needs to retire. Go spend your days reading the newspaper and eating at Big Lou's," Norma kids.

Donovan laughs, then a rumbling under his bony ribs sounds loudly. It was a type of muscle memory for him. His stomach contracts, and he automatically heads to Big Lou's. Nearly every damn day since Norma has known him. His habits and routines hardly strayed. Predictable, Norma would say. "I could go for a big burger right now. Want to get out of here and join me at Big Lou's?"

Norma looks up from the screen. That was the last place she and Alex had shared a meal and the scene where her ultimate nightmare began. She is unsure if she is ready. "I can't," she says.

"Come with me. It will be good for you to face this Norma."

Norma digs deeper into her hollowed soul, when comfort strangely fills her. *It might be nice to feel his presence sitting next to me on the bar stool,* she thinks. If it becomes too much, she knows she can always fall back to this enigmatic puzzle here in Donovan's office. It's been a diversion so far.

CHAPTER 14

Norma and Donovan enter Big Lou's, then promptly sit in the same spot her and Alex once sat. Norma can feel Alex with her, touching her hand. Her eyes close, warmth surrounds her. She smiles. Donovan barks as Elizabeth ignores. For years she has greeted him with some wisecrack about his age, his clothes, the intolerable crankiness that is the Donovan she has grown to adore. However, this time her back remains to him. She places his usual order in the kitchen window. He calls for her and she slowly turns. Her deeply sad face alarms him. This is nothing he has ever seen. Immediately he pries. "What's wrong?" Her eyes are swollen, and her face weakened. Life seems to have been ripped from her body, leaving it devoid of its heart.

"My son…he is missing. He was kidnapped from the daycare I told you about. Now I don't know where he is, if he is ok, or if he is alive." Elizabeth begins to break down as she speaks. Donovan stops her mid-sentence.

"When did this happen? Who is looking for him?" Donovan questions.

"Could it be his father?" Norma asks. She rattles off likely theories, hoping for one to stick.

"No," Elizabeth says. "He abandoned me when I said I was pregnant. I haven't seen him since. The daycare told the police that I picked him up and the police have been treating me as if I have something to do with this. I don't know what to do or who to turn to."

This is far from agency matters, but Donovan feels compelled to help. Atropos is the government's most elite team, but this would never be approved by the higher hand that would allow for such a mission. Only the President could approve this. They highly doubt a mere waitress from Big Lou's stressing over her missing four-year-old son would qualify as national security breach or warrant resources taken from the expulsion of a terrorist cell. But then again, Norma has never been one for following protocols or needing the approval of what the higher hand warrants essential. *Her insolence makes her dangerous*, she can still hear Donovan say, then adding: *it will ruin her one day.*

"When do you get off?" Norma asks.

"In an hour," she says. She begins to weep.

Norma grabs a paper napkin and hands it to Elizabeth to absorb her tears. Whether she was still twirling ill over Rick's deplorable disregard of the innocent, or feeling what if it was Alexander, Norma takes her case and says, "Meet us here." She writes the address to a restaurant on Elizabeth's diner pad. It is a restaurant that Norma and Alex had become silent partners in. The same restaurant that she held Donovan at gunpoint for information to Alexander when she was thought to be dead. *To hell with it,* she thinks; with every resource privy to Atropos, they could find Elizabeth's son before any local enforcement could. "Bring everything you have with you. I want names of everyone at that daycare," Norma says. Norma and Donovan rise, leaving Donovan's plate of fries and greasy burger to cool in the kitchen window. They will regroup to be briefed where privacy is certain.

A flicker of hope overcomes Elizabeth as snivels of gratitude speak to Norma. Norma nods, then leaves. Donovan trails behind her, limping quickly to catch up.

CHAPTER 15

"Table for two, Mrs. Veurr?" the hostess asks. "Will Mr. Veurr be joining you?" The hostess smiles, delighted that Norma has returned after so many months of missed creations by the renowned Greek chef Yiorgos, whom Norma had personally chosen. He is Alex's favorite. Norma offered a lot of dough to lure Yiorgos here. "Your usual table?" she asks.

Looking past the rows of round, white linen-draped tables dimly lit by amber candlelight, Norma sees her and Alex's usual table sitting empty, near the rear of the room. "No," she says. The hostess's confusion leaves Norma with no desire to explain Alex's absence or her unwillingness to sit at their normal table. Norma spots a larger table suitable for three with more room for Donovan to rest his shattered leg and cane. She points. "We will take that one."

Donovan slowly edges his way back as his thoughts are taken back to the night Norma last brought him here. They sit as the hostess places a vinyl-bound menu with chef choices on the table in front of Donovan. "You're kidding, right?" He shuffles his body and leg to a comfortable position and raises the menu to read. “You sure are full of surprises.” He studies the words. “Yup. ‘For mine own part, it was Greek to me.’”

“Alex and I bought it about a year after the last time you and I were here…And when did you start quoting Shakespeare?”

“Yeah, I think I still have a bruise on my back from the gun you shoved in me as we walked back to that table…Have you been here since Alex died? Do they know about Alex?”

“No,” she says.

The waitress approaches the table with crystal stemware filled with icy cucumber water. This is a face Norma has never seen. The waitress places the cut glass in front of Norma, then Donovan. Donovan looks oddly at the glass, then to Norma. Norma is amused at Donovan’s disdain for elegance. “There will be one more joining us,” Norma says. The waitress, appearing well aware of Norma’s station at the restaurant, hurries off to promptly return with one more filled glass with thinly sliced cucumber swimming in fresh water.

“Cucumber water? Really?” Donovan says.

“It is a Greek restaurant. Do you expect anything less?” Norma says. She answers her own question as to how he could recite Shakespeare. It was her love for the culture and its mythology. She assumes after over two decades that it’s finally rubbing off on him—and perhaps a few others of the Atropos team.

The waitress returns, precisely setting the third glass in its proper place. “Would you like to wait for the rest of your party to join you?” she asks. Norma nods, signaling for her to leave them until they arrive.

Donovan squints and muddles the pronunciation of the Greek dishes. "I'm not seeing a burger on this menu," he says. He flips the menu over. "And where are the fries?"

Norma's eyes roll as the waitress returns, only to drop off a plate of freshly made Paximadi and feta. This was actually Alex's favorite Greek bread. He favored the twice baked barley rusk, whereas Norma preferred Tsoureki (Greek Easter sweet-bread). Norma can only assume the young hostess failed to mention that Alex would not be joining her. Norma restrains the urge to excuse herself from the table to sternly coach the waitress on the importance of details. This is not her standard.

Donovan waves his hand as he spots Elizabeth hesitantly entering the restaurant and stop at the hostess stand. He can tell she is uneasy by the way she fidgets. Elizabeth follows behind the hostess timidly with her head down, clutching her purse close to her body. She can sense the patrons staring as the smell of greasy cheeseburgers and fried potatoes waft passed them. The prices on the menu here are not what her bank account can afford. As Elizabeth nears the table, Donovan leans forward to slide the chair out.

"Let me," says the hostess. She reaches in front of Elizabeth to place the vinyl menu on the table. "May I take your coat?" She extends her hand, ready to take it.

Elizabeth pulls her tattered coat tighter to her body. "No thank you," she says, mortified to reveal the Big Lou's uniform hidden underneath. "I'm a bit chilly." She sits, studying the fine white cloth that drapes the table, candlelight that flickers soft colors of white, yellow, red, and intricately detailed sterling silver flatware that provides the finishing touch for the properly appointed table. She is certain that this cold metal fork costs more than the cold cash she makes in a week's tips. She'd always dreamed what it would be like to sit at a table like this when watching it on a movie, on a TV show. She mimics the actress and corrects her posture, puts her legs together, and properly places one hand in her lap while the other raises the menu. Norma glances at Elizabeth's unmanicured fingernails. She can recall a time when she was young when her nails were unpolished.

Norma senses Elizabeth's anxiety rising. The waitress returns and Norma orders three chef's specials for tonight's dinner. She knows that explaining the menu will further Elizabeth's embarrassment. As the waitress turns, Norma calls for her. "Please bring the gentleman and myself a glass of Pappy Van Winkle Twenty-Five-Year Reserve, neat." Norma looks to Elizabeth, unsure if bourbon is her liquor of choice. "Do you like bourbon? Or would you prefer something else?

Elizabeth shyly responds, "No thank you. Just water is fine."

"Wait, you're not drinking it with Coke?" Donovan asks.

"One hardly drinks soda with bourbon that costs three hundred dollars an ounce," Norma smiles. "Alex searched hell over to purchase that bottle for our twenty-fifth wedding anniversary. He thought: what better way to celebrate a relationship so rare than a bottle of rare bourbon." She gazes at their usual table and sighs.

Donovan brings Norma back to the table and back to the reason they are there. "What do you have for us?" he asks Elizabeth.

Norma watches Elizabeth squirm in her seat. "I know you must be exhausted and eager to show us what you've brought."

Norma shuffles the basket of bread and feta, glasses of cucumber water, and silverware to the edge of the table, giving Elizabeth room to lay it all out.

Elizabeth reaches in her purse and slowly begins to lay out the police report, daycare contract, and a picture. "This is Charlie," she says as her sadness deepens. She slowly releases the picture onto the table, appearing reluctant to let it go. Norma can feel Elizabeth's suffering pierce her greatly. She proceeds to question.

"How long has he been missing?" Norma asks, knowing the longer he has been gone the harder it will be. She hopes this to be a rescue not a recovery mission.

"It's been two days, five hours, and nineteen minutes since he was last seen on the daycare monitors."

Norma interrupts. "Who has the video?" she asks.

"The police," Elizabeth says, her frustration apparent. "But it's like he just disappears. One second you can see him in the video, then he's gone." She reaches for a tissue from her purse to wipe the tears that are beginning to fall. Since his disappearance, her eyes have never dried. "I don't understand how he can just disappear." Elizabeth retrieves her cell phone and flips through picture after picture, then stops. She brings it close to her face as if able to smell him, feel his face against hers. "This is a picture I took on his first day there. I didn't want to leave him, but I had a shift and was going to be late. I took a goofy selfie of us in front of the daycare so that I could see him while at work." Elizabeth passes her cell phone to Norma.

Norma studies the young boy's face, full of life, happy yet discontent to leave his mother's side. She can see, despite the despair to part, even for just a few hours, the love they have in their hearts for each other. Norma knows that mother's love. Something in the background catches Norma's attention. Quickly admiration of the two switched to alarm at a white male standing, waiting as Elizabeth and Charlie say goodbye. His image is far away and blurry. Norma zooms in for a closer view. Although distorted, Norma thinks she recognizes his face. She looks to Donovan and hands him the cell phone, keeping the picture still zoomed in. "Look at this," she says, alerting him to a startling connection to them. As Donovan zooms in closer, then out, then closer again to be certain, Norma asks, "Have the police seen this?"

Elizabeth takes a second to mull over everything she had given or showed the police. It has been a hellish nightmare that she can't seem to wake from. All the details are beginning to jumble together. "I don't remember," she says.

Norma's idea becomes lucid in Donovan's mind. "What the fuck!" he says. He zooms in again. "It can't be!"

"Who is that man in the background?" Norma asks. Norma signals for Donovan to hand Elizabeth the cell phone to confirm their suspicions. "What is his name?"

Elizabeth takes her turn to zoom in closer, then tries to focus her mind enough to remember. "I only saw him once. It was Charlie's first day there, and I remember him stopping us to give Charlie a high-five. He said he always likes to meet the new kid on the block. He acted really nice and seemed to take an interest in Charlie. I think he was the owner."

"What was his name?" Norma asks, growing more impatient.

Elizabeth is flustered, trying to recall. "I'm trying to remember."

Donovan takes his hand and gently lays it on Elizabeth's. "Take a deep breath," he says. He pats her hand, hoping to calm her enough to pull a name from her hysterical mind. "Just try to think. Do you remember how he introduced himself to Charlie? What was his name?"

Elizabeth suddenly riles. She remembers. "He said his name was Christoph. He had an Italian accent, but I really think it was fake. I think I picked up a northern dialect or somewhere around there. I thought he was just trying to be funny to make Charlie laugh… put him at ease, being it was his first day and all."

Norma and Donovan look at each other with shocked faces. Without taking her eyes off Donovan, Norma asks, "Did he give you a last name?"

"That I remember now. It was Charlie's favorite Marvel character: Wolverine…Logan. Logan was his last name."

Norma immediately rises to her feet and tells Donovan to bring everything Elizabeth brought to the table. "Stay with her and eat. Then make sure she has food to take home. Come to the office as soon as you're done," she says, rushing for the front door.

"Norma," Elizabeth calls out. Norma stops, then turns toward Elizabeth. "Please find my son. Bring him home to me. No matter how."

"We will find him," Norma says, turning to leave.

CHAPTER 16

Norma sits at Donovan's desk, scouring at Chris Logan and the other rugged faces to fill in blank pieces missing to complete the puzzle. She can sense a connection but is still confused as to how they all fit together. How is the cell that attacked Alexander and killed Alex tied to Charlie, a missing boy attending a daycare where Chris Logan was strangely spotted? She grabs the back of her neck and begins to massage the knot out. Her head begins to ache as she strains to unscramble the pieces when a classified article she had seen comes to mind. She has it. Donovan quickly enters, disrupting what is finally flowing freely through her thoughts.

"Why the hell is Chris Logan at a daycare facility? And believed to be the owner?" he asks. Donovan rushes to Norma's side, stalling only to slam the police report, a picture Elizabeth had given him of Charlie, and Norma's to-go meal onto the desk, wafting over the robust smell of garlic and cigar. Her keen senses are too focused on something more robust, more pungent displaying on the screen to notice. He hovers over

Norma, looking at the split screens of all the faces laid out like the opening to a diabolical episode of *The Terrorist Bunch*. Three rows of three pictures with the leader of cell that Norma killed in the Lesser Caucasus five years ago in the middle. Surrounding him is Chris Logan, the terrorist Norma killed at the Lincoln Memorial and the three at the warehouse, the younger doppelganger Atropos spotted in Iraq, and question marks for the missing faces needed to complete this picture.

"I think I have it…At least the *why*," she says. A screen is minimized and a new search engine is opened for Norma to enter credentials. She remembers watching as Rick navigated the internet searching for a dark web just before the devil's breath took him away. It is a world wide web that is privy to a select few, and she needs to be cautious that cookies aren't left, trailing deadly pests back to her. She needs his passwords to enter. Norma opens the top desk drawer and reaches under. She takes out a small, tightly sealed container. She opens it and removes a contact lens from its solution. She places it on her eyeball. Norma shifts to the other monitor and places her eye to the camera. It scans, opening the cloud of zipped files she will need. The keyboard is pounded rapidly with IDs, passwords, IP addresses, gateways stored and sealed. She turns back to the monitor and in a few strokes of the keys, she enters Rick's secret passageway to the web's backdoor. She types the ID and password Rick used, then hits enter with hopes that the one in charge has left it accessible.

"Yup! You sure are full of surprises… What is this?" Donovan asks.

"After the devil's breath rendered him powerless to resist, Rick showed me how he was able to go from white hat to black hat to confirm where and who had Alexander. Before he was dead I took his eye and had it replicated in that lens. I knew there would be times we would still need him." For a second, Norma's skin crawls with the idea that Rick's DNA could be running in her blood. It pleases her to know that it is not, and it was by her hand that the ominous director's term was ended. Now the only remnants of him are embedded in that lens or contained in an urn on top of a mantle.

She's in. Norma switches from white hat to black hat and spies all through the spider web, searching to remember. "There it is," she says. Norma rises out of the chair to allow Donovan to take a seat, then takes her turn to stand behind him. She leans in to click open the file. "Look at this." They speed through the pages. A link is hit and they enter a live room filled with shadows, except for one.

"We need to call Atropos into the meeting room now," Donovan says.

Alexander and David enter the office still lagged from their travel back into US Eastern Time zone. They yawn, forcing oxygen to their brains to wake for just enough time to de-brief, then to take a shower and get some dry clothes on. For Alexander, maybe even an extra second to steal a taste of Nyx's sweet lips. He begins to text to see if Nyx is home but suddenly stops when looking to his mother. "You two look intense," he says. He notices the stress in her eyes. "Are we headed back out?" he asks.

Norma looks up to see David moving closer to her for a view at whatever is on the screen that has them two so concerned. She quickly halts him. "Stay over there," she says, unwilling to make him a part of her cyber trespass against the only one who could remove her from Atropos.

"Get the team assembled into the briefing room," Donovan says.

"What's going on?" David asks. "I'm assuming we are headed to hell."

"I'll explain soon. Get Atropos together," Norma says, pushing them out the door.

CHAPTER 17

"Listen up!" Donovan yells. "Take a seat. This won't take long."

Alexander and David take their seats to the front as Xavier and the remaining team sits behind them anxious to hear what vital mission may lie ahead. Xavier leans forward to rest his head onto Alexander's shoulder. "Let's spoon, princess. I'm tired," Xavier says.

Alexander shrugs him off and looks back, laughing at Xavier's madness. "What?!"

Xavier puckers his lips. "You know you'd rather have these lips than your little girlfriend's. I saw her sexy little ass coming out of your building the other day. When do I get to meet her?"

"Enough, Xavier!" Norma demands from the front. "Pay attention."

Donovan takes the minute needed to load up the large screen on the wall. The layout of terrorist faces appears. The Atropos men become intrigued as to what revelation has occurred within the time they spent napping on the stealth helicopter ride home. The picture of Charlie and the little girl at the hotel in Iraq pulls up to the side of the layout leaving them even more so curious. *What does this little boy and little girl have to do with marked terrorists?* plays at the same time in Atropos minds.

"It is with a reliable resource we believe that this cell you men just retrieved intel on is connected to using child trafficking and organ harvesting to fund their cause. Without elaborating the source is has been reported that those Jihad in Lesser Caucuses used money from drugs and child trafficking to support terrorism. We have seen the auctions… Chris Logan was from Detroit. Detroit is one of the cities used in the US for trafficking kids stolen from all over the states. Of course, you guessed it, Washington, DC, is one of the top… They are sold to pedophiles in Africa, Asia, Europe, and yes, even powerful people inside the United States." Norma points to a photo. "You see that little boy? His name is Charlie. We're going to find him! Time is ticking!"

Norma walks away from the podium and sits next to David allowing Donovan to take over. David can see that this mission, unlike any other, has her tense. Donovan goes over the intel taken from the report and known undergrounds used to smuggle the children. "Before we bulldoze these tunnels we need more intel and fast. It will not be easy. There are tunnels all across the US and into Mexico and there are at least two hundred and fifty thousand kids smuggled from within those tunnels alone that are sold into the child sex trafficking market. Worldwide, over two million. Unfortunately, it's the fastest-growing criminal enterprise in the world, and this terrorist cell is part of it." Donovan points to the framed

X'd out faces, then to the blank squares with question marks in the middle. "We need to know who these are. If we find them, we find the boy!"

Xavier agitates wide awake and loudly interrupts. "Let me go. When do we go? I'll kill those sick motherfuckers! Why haven't we heard about this?"

"Norma and I have our speculation as to who covers this up and why there isn't media hype over it. The depths to which this goes will unsettle you. But for now, let's focus on finding this little boy and any other child along the way," Donovan says.

"How the hell are they stealing these kids? How did this boy get kidnapped?" Alexander asks.

"By the intel we saw, there is a prolific number of ways these kids are snatched. Charlie was taken from an operation posing as a daycare. Norma spotted Chris Logan in the boy's picture and after watching what happened in Iraq with the little girl and the doppelganger, she made the connection. Other ways that we saw reported were baby and home security cams being hacked, child rehab centers, homeless kids on the streets, from neighborhoods, private schools, high-end hotels, and, sadly, their own parents. We saw footage of a van stopping in a back alley and the asphalt opening up to an underground tunnel below. A teenage girl was shoved down it after an Amber Alert was issued… That was in Texas."

Secret underground tunnels this team knows all too well. How others are able to engineer under the nose of Americans they have no idea.

"Again, this won't be easy. These people will not give up that easy. These kids can be worth big money…anywhere between four thousand and fifty thousand each… And this time, men, for the first time, we will be fighting on… our own soil."

Alexander, David, Lander, Kosmo, Stefen, Xavier, Raiden, Vali, Milo, and Nick all look to each other rearing for a chance to spray heavily, terminating anyone willing to spoil such innocence through whichever underground tunnel they may find them in. By Norma's face, she may feel obliged to join them.

Norma speaks up. "First things first. I am sending you guys back to Iraq to capture the doppelganger. Except Alexander and David. You two will stay behind and help prepare for the mission ahead to search for Charlie. It'll also give me the little time I need to extinguish some fires. We don't need any distractions. I will need focus. Xavier, you take lead. If successful capturing the doppelganger, we should be able to extract more information that we need in order to save time hunting. These groups have a tendency to close one tunnel, only to make another. If we are going to save this boy before he is lost deep underground, we will need the intel to penetrate from behind instead of barreling forward."

A smart remark, wise crack to Norma about penetrating from behind would any other time be expected from Xavier. This time he sits quiet.

Norma rises from her chair. "For the rest of you, go to The World Renaissance Hotel to rest up for a couple of hours while the chopper refuels and I find out if we are cleared—or if we go rogue," she says. As she begins to leave David follows closely behind her. With fate uncertain he feels he must tell her before his chance is gone.

"Norma," David calls. Norma stops in the hallway and turns to face him. "We need to talk."

"It's not the time, David," she says, turning and walking away. She is not prepared to pull the trigger on the fire extinguisher just yet.

David commands his tone speaking louder. "Norma stop! We need to talk."

Norma releases a deep breath, then turns. "What? What, David?" she asks, fearing that he is about to make a plea for Alexander. It is no secret that they were in deep conversation sitting on those rocks in the middle of the Iraq Mountain. Alexander may have muted their words, but Norma could understand the language their bodies were saying. After meeting Nyx, seeing the way Alexander looked at her, and being that his best friend, his confidant, his father was dead; Alexander went to the next one in line that he could inevitably trust. David stands mustering the words as his longing blue eyes stare deep into hers. She's taken aback as she notices him gazing admirably at her hair, her body, her ivory skin. "What," she says.

"I know you love me…" David hesitates preferring to expose his weakness to one of those men on the screen than to expose it to Norma right here, right now. "Do you still feel anything like you did for me, before Alex?"

Oh my God, this is worse, Norma thinks. She would rather it had been about Alexander and Nyx. She is definitely not prepared for this.

David sees the horror on her face and switches to different matter of hearts. He tries to cover up his true intentions. "I'm asking for you to remember how we were then; how you and Alex were." By the relief on Norma's face, he thinks he is in the clear. His true feelings will have to wait. "I remember when Alex and you met. How Alex looked at you. I saw that same look in Alexander's face for Nyx. He is in love with this girl and I think she feels the same way. He came to me for help. To get your approval."

"Not the time," Norma says, turning to walk away. "I will speak with Alexander later." Norma rushes to put distance between them.

"God damn it, Norma. Don't walk away from me." David watches as she continues down the hall. "The agency couldn't stop you. You won't be able to stop Alexander and Nyx," echoes loudly within the walls. David stands, rejected to any of his notions.

CHAPTER 18

Alexander makes it to the front doors of his building and stops. He looks around. Part of him wants to rush through into the lobby while the stronger part urges him to wait. He has changed into dry clothes but is desperate for a quick shower, then a special visitor to come knocking. Norma has not given him much time to return, so he will take all that was allotted to see her. Still, he takes a second to look all around for Mr. Henry. A sick feeling comes across him when finally he mumbles, "There he is." He sees Mr. Henry shuffling back as fast as waning legs and stiff, crackling knees will allow. Mr. Henry stops close to the valet station.

"I was starting to get worried," Alexander says.

"Oh, I'm all right," says Mr. Henry. He fondly pats Alexander on the back. Breathy, he adds, "How are you tonight, sir?"

"Please stop calling me that. You don't need to call me sir." Alexander flashes a smile, then puts his warm arm around Mr. Henry's freezing neck. "I told you, people need to call you sir." He removes his arm and as desperate as he is for more time to have Nyx wrapped around him, he sees that the deep wrinkles seem to carve a map on Mr. Henry's face, proving that his journey is about to end. Alexander notices that Mr. Henry's long coat hangs a tad lower off his burdened shoulders. He has become thinner, weaker with each day passing. "How is your grandbaby?" he asks.

"Not too good," Mr. Henry says. His grin is as forced as his cheer to the residents walking past him as he welcomes them home. If for one second they would see him as Alexander does, they would see the old man that tends to their whiniest whims was darkening with each sunset that passed. "We're waiting to see if this specialist doctor will help her at Children's Hospital. He doesn't take Medicaid, so I don't think she's gonna get in."

Alexander looks at his service pin proudly placed on his lapel. "Well, we still have a chance for that winning lottery, remember? Hope!"

"Oh, Mr. Alexander, my days of hoping to win are gone," he says. The bleak outcome is undeniable. He has accepted it. "I figure it's best I just come to work for as long as they let me and get a paycheck to help my grandbaby the best I can." Mr. Henry feels his fate has been determined by someone higher than Lady Luck.

Alexander disagrees. He decides that he will hold hope for Mr. Henry until the next time he sees him and all is well. His guarded heart was unbounded for the brittle man.

"Why are you down here wasting time talking to me?" Mr. Henry teases. "I know a certain young lady that can't wait to see you. You know she goes out of her way every day to see how I'm doing. Nice girl she is," he says. Mr. Henry budges Alexander to a more promising subject. "When are you gonna make that nice girl yours?"

Alexander's teeth shine brighter than the moon illuminating through the night's dark sky. *Nyx,* he thinks, *Mrs. Veurr.* Norma comes to mind. He shivers. "See you later, Mr. Henry."

Alexander rushes through the door, throwing his keys onto the coffee table. By her text she unwillingly agreed to the few minutes he requested to rid Iraq from his body. She has been eager to talk to him, touch him, and see him. Willingly, he knew it to be necessary. He thinks if this was to go where he hopes, eventually she will need to learn who he truly is. That mixed martial arts was not practiced solely in a safe dojo and that the wounds on his body did not come from some fierce competitor. One day soon his mind feels he will have what his heart desires.

One by one, clothes are pulled off his body until the shower steams, ready to wash away the soggy day. Dried cakey mud softens as the warm water runs down his chiseled body. Alexander wastes no time washing, then rinsing the remnants of Iraq down the drain. He opens the shower door and hears a knock at the door. Thick, cushy, Egyptian cotton wraps low around his waist, then a corner tucks into the side. He briskly brushes his teeth, gurgles a mouthful of mint rinse, sweeps his hair back, then looks to the mirror for approval. He can see his mother's image looking back and hears the Atropos vow. Louder knocks bring him back to her. "Nyx," he calls out.

Alexander is barely able to open the door when Nyx lunges onto him, nearly knocking the towel off his waist. "I've missed you," she says. She rises on the tip of her toes to wrap her arms around his neck. "We need to talk." By the way excitement is clearly showing from under his towel, talking is not quite what Alexander has in mind right now. "I can't wait to tell you something." He chuckles at the sight of her excitement. Perhaps not the same as his but amusing all the same.

"Slow down," Alexander laughs. "I know I need to tell you something, too. First—" His hands softly cradle her chin "—I have missed you," he says. He leans down to feel her warm, soft lips against his. This is what he has been craving. "I needed that."

Nyx pulls back, ready to explode with the words she's done so well to hold in. "We need to talk." Her glossed lips part, impatient to share her secret, but Alexander blocks them with his tongue. He kisses her until the taste of berries has long been gone. He can't take anymore. Whatever she has to say must wait. He must feel her, all of her. His lips guide her to the bedroom. He undresses her until her nipples appear as hard as he is. The towel is thrown to the side of the bed. She slowly lies back as his body stays pressed against hers. His hands glide under her arms until they reach the back of her neck. He firmly holds her neck as he slides inside and is swallowed by her wet vertical lips. Her sweet scented perfume fuses with the sweat beading from their bodies. His explosion cannot be contained. As he slips deeper into her he says, "I love you." This is the first time Nyx has ever heard Alexander say it. His words have touched her deeper than his flesh, then came the crying, in a sort of sobbing monologue.

"What's wrong?" he says.

"You have never said that to me before. I've been waiting." She can see his relief that now his soul is as bare as his body. Her eyes watch as Alexander falls to her side. She can tell he is exhausted and contemplates sharing her news. It would make this moment all the more epic. His hand strokes her face, and in seconds she can hear his breathing slow and his arm go heavy over her chest. "Alexander," she quietly calls. Her fingers glide up and down his arm as he sleeps. Nyx traces the scar that Mackenzie had left just before he died and wonders where it came from. He would never tell her. She outlines his strong jaw line and his ideal nose and marvels at the long black lashes that rest just above his cheeks. His beckoning body, his sharp features, his alluring soul. *He is perfect,* she thinks. After minutes of brushing her fingers through his black wavy hair, Nyx begins to drift.

Alexander startles awake, jerking Nyx up from falling deep into the sandman's welcoming arms. "What time is it?" He looks to his watch and sees that it has been only thirty minutes. His stomach rumbles and growls, demanding food. "Want to go get something to eat?" She wants to say no, we really need to talk, but she chooses for another time. As they dress, Alexander remembers. "What did you need to tell me?"

"It can wait." Nyx reaches down and grabs her pants off the floor. One leg slides in, then the other, and suddenly she stops and sits on the bed. "Alexander," she calls, then waits for his attention. "What did your mother say about me, about us?"

Alexander has no desire to delve into that right now. And frankly he is no longer concerned. Nyx is who he wants. Why can't he be allowed to have what his parents had? She may not be a part of them but Alexander is confident it will work. "She wants me to focus on my career," he says. That sounded weird even to him. He's not sure if it's the "career" part or that he just portrayed Norma as a helicopter mom. She is stealthy, just not in that way. Alexander agrees that not having Nyx in his life is safer for them both. But every fiber in his being tells him that she is the one. "Let's just have a great night. We can share our big news over dinner…Oh, I wanted to tell you earlier… we just found out we're headed back out." Nyx was not a fan of his travels but would never stand in his way of his career, whatever that might be.

"No fair. I just got you back," she says, teasing.

Alexander leans down and kisses her forehead. "I know but I'll be back soon." They head for the door when Alexander realizes he was about to forget something that he had arranged days earlier. He leaves Nyx at the door and disappears back into the bedroom. Metal screeches open, then clanks shut. He reappears with an envelope and follows her out the door.

"What is that?" she asks.

"Hope," he says. They smile.

Alexander and Nyx walk out the door that Mr. Henry is holding wide open for them.

"Enjoy your evening, Mr. Alexander," Mr. Henry says.

Alexander is smirking. He looks to Nyx as she shines the sweetest smile back. Mr. Henry sees the two young loves beaming at each other as happiness fills the bitter air around them. He perceives their blissful glow from the visible love that they have for one another. Alexander stops and reaches into his jacket pocket to retrieve the envelope that he almost forgot. It has a picture of a lottery ticket on it. Printed and labeled with big bold letters: **H O P E**. He hands it to Mr. Henry. This is the reason for their broad smiles.

"What's this, Mr. Alexander?" he asks. Confusion riddles his face. He stares at the addressed envelope, attempting to figure out what Alexander is up to now. A bunch of chances stuffed in this envelope with HOPE that one wins big, Mr. Henry guesses. He is touched by Alexander's kindness. "Oh, Mr. Alexander, you didn't have to do this," he says, remembering the morning he wished and hoped for luck to win the mega millions ticket. Mr. Henry would be tickled pink if he scratches to reveal he had won five dollars. A warm pastry would complement the hotel's coffee nicely on this cold evening.

Alexander struggles to contain himself as Nyx looks on, excited. "Open it," he says. Alexander nudges Mr. Henry's trembling hand. "Come on, open it!"

Mr. Henry peels open the envelope and peeks in. It's not what he expected. There's but one thing in there, and it's not un-sequenced, quick-pick numbers printed on a small square piece of paper. It's not a colorful paper card with numbers ready to be scratched off to reveal if it's a winner. This paper is longer and folded, and if he had to guess, it's a check. Mr. Henry pulls it out. "Mr. Alexander, what did you do?" he asks. Christmas is long past, and Alexander's generous bonus had been more than enough. Some residents gave a fruit basket, some gave a Christmas card with a twenty-dollar bill stuffed in it, while others just offer a halfhearted Merry Christmas;

but not Alexander. Every year he has given Mr. Henry a Christmas card with no less than five thousand dollars. Money well-earned, if you ask Alexander. The check opens and Mr. Henry's eyes read the numbers. His expression is blank as he reads numbers backward. He counts six zeros, then a one. The numbers refuse to register.

Nyx begins to sniffle while trying her best not to ruin perfectly good makeup.

"I thought you could use some HOPE. Dad had a healthy insurance policy when he died, and I still have more than I need from when Mom sold her company over five years ago. I want to spend it where it will matter. You matter, Mr. Henry. Your granddaughter matters."

The numbers finally register. "I can't take this," Mr. Henry says. He shoves the check back into the envelope and hands it to Alexander. His head shakes side to side, saying no, no, then definitely no. He is overwhelmed. "I can't take this!"

"You will," Alexander says, pushing Mr. Henry's hand away from him. He straightens Mr. Henry's forty-year service pin. "Look at it like this pin...You deserve it." Alexander zips his jacket, then grins at Nyx as she desperately straightens her face. He takes his finger and wipes away smeared mascara from under her eyes.

"Isn't she beautiful," he says. Alexander turns back to Mr. Henry and continues to delight. He is not done yet. "I also talked to an old college friend of mine from George Washington University. He is a resident at John Hopkins Children's Center. He got me in contact with the doctors there who will now be handling your granddaughter's case and treatment from here on out. As a personal favor for me...well more for my mother. She has donated quite generously to their children's ward. I think your granddaughter will be in excellent hands now."

Mr. Henry trembles, not from the cold sky, not for the cruel joke Father Time or Mother Nature has played on his aging body, not for the fear that's stolen his dreams of who his grandbaby might one day be, but for the kindness, the kindness that will ultimately change his and his granddaughter's stars. He shakes Alexander's hand, accepting hope.

Alexander grabs Nyx's hand and begins to walk off. He stops to look back at Mr. Henry. "I'm going to miss you." Alexander and Nyx walk off, starting their new journey together, leaving the old man time, whatever that maybe, to spend with his one true love.

Alexander shields and protects Nyx from the people walking aimlessly on the sidewalk. "Alexander," she says, overwhelmed that now must be the time. "I know you can't tell me everything about what you or your mom, or David, or the guys do, and I know I'm not supposed to ask questions...I'm fine with that. I get it. You're some kind of secret government military, and I'm just some prima ballerina who doesn't belong in your world...and seeing that your mom isn't too keen on this relationship, on me..."

"Is this what you wanted to talk to me about?" Alexander asks. He is uncertain after Mr. Henry why this is so important that she would want to stray from such a breathtaking moment.

Nyx stops cold, shivering. "You said your mom was protective. That she is the one to call if anything ever went wrong..."

Nyx stalls looking to the frosty air for words. "Would she be this protective if…?" Once more, the words frighten her to silence. She tugs Alexander away from the people as they rush by.

"What?" Alexander says, impatient for Nyx to tell him what has been so damn hard for her to say. "Is everything okay? You're not making any sense," he persists. "Nyx! What's wrong with you?"

"Will she be this protective when her bloodline comes from someone whom she doesn't feel belongs?" Nyx gently rubs her belly, then looks to Alexander. "Her grandbaby?… Alexander, I'm pregnant."

The cars, the pedestrians, the world, all stand still to Alexander as he, too, stands motionless on the sidewalk.

CHAPTER 19

Atropos jumps out of the stealth helicopter that is perched at the newly constructed international airport near Duhok, quietly spinning its blades as it stands by, idling for the team to return. The abandoned construction site airport is in the town of Simele, near the main road that connects Iraq and Turkey. The team will need to travel the 8.7 miles in the arranged cattle wagon to the far top side of the mountain in Duhok, where the doppelganger was last seen in the town just at the bottom on the other side.

"Move your fat ass," Xavier says, pushing Raiden to the side for first dibs in the wagon. "Doesn't your name mean 'God of thunder' in Latin?" he says. His head shakes at the idea that Norma has ruined him with everything Greek. She is apparently rubbing off on more than just Donovan. "I really can't believe I know that." He shoves Raiden harder, pushing him. "Move your thunder thighs," he says.

Xavier steals shotgun and places his customized automatic rifle between his crimped up legs. At six feet four inches, the back of the wagon may have been a better choice. With two bench seats, one on each side, and plenty of leg room in between, he would not feel like a stuffed sardine in this metal box. But this is where he believes he belongs. The leader's seat. Xavier fidgets with the little computer screen on the watch that would traditionally be reserved for Alexander. "You bitches better listen to me," he says. "I'm the leader this time. You follow me. Get your asses back there." He shuts the door.

Headsets are secured firmly on top of their heads, then a third eye is attached. Simultaneously back in Washington, DC, eight visuals pop up on the screen. Channels are secured. "Clear." Norma's voice waves crisp into their ears. The men listen as Norma instructs them what to do. Thumbs rise for the third eye to see. Conversations stream through the private channel.

"Didn't we just leave here?" Raiden asks. It's unusual for them to return so soon. However, it's unusual for them to leave with the soil not soaked in their enemy's blood. "This is all too déjà vu. Better yet, déjà poop!"

"Keep up your whining and I'll turn this car around and go home," Xavier kids.

Norma and Donovan begin to believe that putting Xavier in the lead was not the wisest choice. A skilled warrior, an Atropos original... that he is. He is also hotheaded, easy to cock, and prefers the custom assault rifle for its velocity—the ability to splatter the human body into pink mist. The remaining Atropos team members chose a less dramatic death for their targets. This "lumberjack," as Dorian used to call him, welcomes the gore.

The men sit in the covered wagon as sandy dirt clouds the air. As their bodies bounce with each dip in the road, they prepare for the mission ahead. Rain begins to tap the canvas top.

"You've got to be fucking kidding," Vali says. "My balls just got dry and thawed out from the last time we were here." Vali, an Arizonan cowboy at heart, replaced Ares to become the one who loathed the cold the most. If Ares was still alive, they would have much in common. But now, only Alexander can see Ares, as he haunts his dreams of the day the doppelganger's father took Ares' head, all in the name of jihad. As told, the day Norma, Alex, and Donovan rescued Atropos from capture in the Lesser Caucasus. Xavier has no intent on needing rescue today. He is confident in his intent to capture the leader's son and make him talk, and if Norma allows, make the doppelganger join his father's side in Jahannam (Islam's hell).

"Ninety-nine terrorist jihads on the wall, ninety-nine terrorist jihads, take one day down splatter him around, ninety-eight terrorist jihads on the wall," Xavier sings.

"Shut up!" sounds loudly from the team bouncing in the back of the wagon.

Xavier looks to the Iraqi driver as the Iraqi driver looks bizarrely at Xavier. "I don't think they like my singing." The driver's eyes widen, surveying Xavier, hands resting loosely on the steering wheel, guiding the wagon to the top of the mountain. Xavier listens as Norma scorns the importance of this mission. He knows just as she knows this has always been his way. The truck pulls to the side of the road and Atropos men jump to fall into position. In a single line, with Milo in lead, the men move down the rugged mountain with rifles in hand and pistols tucked safely to the side of their waist. They trail closely together following a tree line for cover as they patrol barren rocky hills.

"Milo," Vali calls forward. Milo turns around to see Vali pointing to his boot knife. It has loosened from its sheath nearly falling out. Milo stops and bends to adjust as Vali passes him. Xavier walks up, kicks Milo off balance, then passes. "Dick," Milo grumbles as Xavier snickers ahead. Atropos brothers they are despite Xavier, along with David, having more than two and a half decades of deadly missions under their utility ammo belts.

The rain clouds have since vanished to reveal that the sun is beginning to set. The noises of the wildlife continue to halt them, then take cover. As each time is confirmed safe to continue, tense muscles begin to build up. They have gone far enough for now. Eyes are planted on the hotel the doppelganger was last seen. They hunker down and wait for the sun to retreat below the horizon. It is seven PM here and the Kurds are retreating, as well, into their homes for a plate of lamb stuffed with spicy rice or Dolma (stuffed spiced rice wrapped in grape leaves) with a glass of tea.

"What a beautiful sunset to start such a doomed night," Raiden says, watching as the rich, bold, fiery colors surrender to the darkening sky. He secures the rifle between his bent knees and takes the right tactical glove off to adjust the Kevlar vest that has shifted on the hike down. "It's fucking cold here in the winter," he says. He blows warm breaths onto his fingers, then quickly places the glove back on. The Tigris River is chilling the night's air even more so.

"You Florida boys can't take the cold, either," Xavier says. He expects that out of Vali, but now Raiden whining over a little frost. "You guys are a bunch of pussies. I don't know why you cry over frozen balls when you don't seem to have any." Lander, Kosmo, and Stefen laugh. Nick, the youngest and newest member of Atropos, is still uncertain of Xavier. He has not had the years that they do with Xavier to know that Xavier's savage personality is solely for those that one would agree deserve it. For the innocent, Xavier is secretly the softest of the bunch. Perhaps this is why Norma gave him the lead. She suspects they share similar scars from childhood memories. That the scars on their backs tell a similar tale. A tale that will make Xavier invaluable to these innocent children. So Norma imagines. Now only if he can capture the doppelganger and bring him to her in one piece…this Norma hopes.

Stefen spots what he thinks is the sedan the doppelganger was last seen in. Norma confirms. They watch to see if he is in the car. The car pulls up and stops near the valet canopy. An unknown face, assumingly local, gets out with a child held tightly in his hand. The little dark skinned boy looks closely to the same age as the blond, fair-skinned girl from before. They would guess five, maybe six. He is hurried into the hotel, visibly in distress. Xavier moves down, closer to the town's edge. The team cautiously follows, careful not to be seen. This will be as far as they can go without detection. Eight men in black tactical gear, bulging utility belts, headsets with a third eye, pistols swaying on hips, and automatic rifles gripped tightly in hands doesn't necessarily blend in with the local men that are in either muted earth tones or colorful baggy pants with a plain shirt, vest, or jacket, and sometimes even a sash around their waist. Atropos looks as if ready for war, although that they are not. All they want is the doppelganger—then perhaps the cell with him, and the child or children who have been obviously stolen. Xavier wonders how these people don't see what's right in front of their eyes until he remembers asking Norma that same question about the people on his own homeland soil. The same local man who entered the hotel can be seen leaving, this time will a kid that appears older. This dark-skinned girl looks to be twelve. She staggers, stumbling, then is shoved into the car before him.

Here in this peaceful town of Duhok, a Kurdistan region with an abundance of tourism, sits a terrorist child trafficking cell. It kills Xavier and the men to sit idle. They want to storm the hotel and retrieve every innocent soul held captive in there. Norma comes in clear that this mission is to capture the doppelganger with hopes of finding Charlie. Xavier's middle finger rises up to the third eye. Norma knows that is not intended for her. She, too, would like nothing more than to storm with them. "Steady, Xavier," Norma says.

The outside becomes as black as the doppelganger's heart, and the men begin to anticipate an all-nighter is inevitable. Worse, they will trek back to the helicopter empty handed with no doppelganger and leaving quite the cliffhanger. The Atropos team listens to Norma as they watch her words play out in front of them. The Iraqi driver has traded the cattle wagon for an SUV and is parked in front of the hotel. He can be seen stepping out and looking toward them. They assume he is on the agency's payroll, and Norma is using the terrorist cell angle for approval to have boots on the ground. *Intel con-*

firmed Charlie was here, so where the hell is he? Xavier wants to know.

Atropos watches as check-ins flock in. Not a single sighting of the doppelganger's brown-skin face with dark-lined eyes and dark bushy brows. He is unmistakable by the limp in his walk; from what intel offered, it was a result of a failed Al-Qaeda attack on US soldiers. The team perks when the sedan returns. This time the same noticeable potbellied and pudgy-nose man gets out of the car alone, then stands near the canopy to draw the last puffs from his cigarette.

"I thought smoking was banned here," Nick says. Norma explains that not only is Al-Qaeda funded by drugs and child trafficking, but it has multimillion-dollar operations even in the United States, smuggling cigarettes from the low-tax southern states to the high-tax northern states, Detroit, Michigan, Chris Logan's hometown, being one of them. It is easier and doesn't carry the same risks and draconian penalties as illicit drugs do, she further explains. Now that the night cloaks their position, Norma instructs Xavier to move the men in closer but warns him to heed caution.

"Woman, I got this," Xavier says. He grabs Lander by the bill of his cap and pulls his face closer to his. He looks into the third eye and blows a kiss. "Kidding, boss," he says.

Atropos moves quietly down the remaining hundred feet to the edge of town, stopping just shy of the hotel. This hotel was picked for its side and rear on the edge, out-of-the-way location. If compromised the terrorist could easily head for the mountains only to be intercepted at the top, then quickly shuffled to the construction site at the vacant airport. It was because of this that Atropos chose this path. Xavier resumes eye contact with the Iraqi driver. It is at this time that Xavier's appetite proves hungrier than most. The driver nods, signaling he has a visual of their target leaving the reception area. Norma gives the order: "In five." The driver opens the doors to the SUV as Atropos moves in. As they round the corner the doppelganger tries to take flight, but Raiden chases and catches him. Xavier and Lander quickly run to Raiden's aid as the other Atropos men circle the SUV with rifles waving, daring a fight. The locals scatter, taking shelter behind closed doors. Xavier grabs the doppelganger by the neck and forcefully shoves him into the SUV. Atropos wastes no time to load in, slamming doors closed, and then ordering the driver to "Move, move, move!"

Xavier looks back through the rear window at the hotel, eager to return for the children left behind.

"Another team is on the way. Stay the course, Xavier," Norma says.

CHAPTER 20

Norma falls back into her chair and runs her hands over her head, then removes the headset, relieved that the doppelganger is being escorted on a helicopter to Washington, DC. She will have around twelve hours to prepare his accommodations. Norma hopes to offer the same hospitality as the doppelganger's father did to Alexander and Atropos in the Lesser Caucasus or his henchman Chris Logan did at the warehouse. After a quick break for a late lunch, she will be all too obliged to make sure she does not disappoint. She wonders if the doppelganger will have the stomach for what she plans to serve. David enters the office desiring a little time before the pending mayhem of interrogations and chasing terrorists in tunnels, bunkers, or back alleyways is in motion.

"That's a sinister smile," he says.

Norma rises out of the chair and steps toward him. "We got him." She stops at the antique cabinet near David's leg and flips the wood panel up to reveal a mini bar. Two shot glasses, then a crystal decanter of bourbon is taken out and placed on the desk. "I am looking forward to spending a little time with him," she says. The bourbon is poured into the shot glasses. Norma hands David one, then raises her filled shot glass. "*Vindicta*" (Latin, Vengeance). Her thirst will soon be quenched.

"*Vindicta*," David says. They shoot it back, then place the glasses back onto the desk. "Where's Donovan? You actually let the old guy out of your sight now?"

Norma's blue eyes narrow as porcelains peek out from their natural shades. She notices David staring. "Donovan is with Elizabeth, consulting and seeing if she has anything else that could help us," she says. Norma sees that David's eyes have not left hers. She abruptly breaks away and returns to screens that she swears are part of her retina now. For the last couple of days she has spent long hours peering through dark webs. David corners the desk and partially leans back to sit against the mahogany desk ledge next to Norma. The outline of his washboard abs show by the tight, clinging shirt he is wearing. He sits near her head. She can feel his warm energy.

David marvels at how the ceiling light shimmers off her long raven hair. How, even with a vial of THR shot into her thigh, after countless knife wounds, fist wounds, a grazed bullet… her angelic face and mesmerizing eyes could still be so flawless. Statue-worthy one could say. "Perfect," David says.

With eyes still immersed into the screens, Norma never turns away as she feels David eyes are sharply studying her. "Stop it," she says.

David pulls, gliding her chair closer to him. He reaches down to take her hand, then pulls her up and out of the seat. "Alex would want you to move on," he says softly, staring deep into her eyes. For the first time in over two and half decades, David is getting his time, his chance. "He would approve." Norma pulls away, so David pulls her harder into him. He is certain that if she would feel his chest, she would feel the love he has kept for her for all these years. The same love she felt so many years ago—before Alex. David slowly leans in, testing how far she is willing to go until his lips press against hers. She doesn't refuse him, but she doesn't encourage him either. She just stands with her eyes closed, arms relaxed by her sides, and knees weakening as her lips begin to part. Her body begins to throb and ache, but for whom she is not certain. Norma opens her eyes and for the first time in a long time, she really sees David. The eighteen-year-old David that she met when they were young GIs; the David that she shielded, then revenged, when pinned down; the David she wept for by his bedside in the hospital when he was critically injured.

"You can love two people," he whispers softly in her ear. David pulls her body in closer, tighter, and feels the chain links break free from around his heart. His blood now flows freely, fiercely for her. He no longer feels a need to guard his heart. His words are hushed as his lips have long been yearning to taste her. In the last two and half decades, they have spoken enough. Now is his chance to silence words and feel all of her. The passion in his kiss is as if he's siphoning the pain from deep within her soul. As her body presses close to his, he moves his hands down to slowly unbutton her blouse. One by one her buttons begin to open and his anticipation mounts, ready to burst. David watches as she stands and closes her eyes once again as if to heighten each sensual touch to her body. He cradles her breast while tenderly kissing, then nibbling, behind her ear. He hopes it's still an erogenous zone for her, and by the way her body is responding, he thinks he has remembered correctly. The heat generating from their bodies, is making more than blood rise and flow. He slows down and backs off slightly, then once again he feels her lips against his just to prove this was real and not just one of his dreams. "I love you," he whispers in a longing breath. With eyes closed and her heart racing, Norma wraps her arms tightly around him. Calmness suddenly comes over her.

"*Amica mea*," slowly escapes her parted lips. "Alex," she calls out. The door wildly opens, startling them. Her eyes open wide.

"Alexander," David says, covering Norma as she anxiously buttons up her blouse.

Alexander can feel the steamy air. "I'll come back," he says, glancing back at his mother.

"Alexander," Norma yells. She finishes the last button, straightens herself up. "Alexander," she calls out louder. He obediently returns. A smirk is on his face, and Norma secretly finds it humorous that Alexander finds this awkwardness amusing, so she thinks. *I take their bond is tight. He approves,* Norma thinks. *Or perhaps it's amusing to him that this time he's the one interrupting.* "What do you need?" she asks. The excitement, the joy that is all over his face for whatever news he is so eager to share, reminds her of Alexander as a child on Christmas morning ready to open pretty wrapped boxes tagged with his name. He is beyond happy, ecstatic. Norma is certain this is not regarding a new lead on a missing boy, child trafficking, doppelganger terrorist, or the hellish mission that lies ahead. A distant idea comes forth. The only smile that she has seen on his face lately has Nyx somewhere in the sentence. Norma is beginning to wonder why she hasn't nixed Nyx. His smile looks dangerous.

"This is not the time," Alexander says.

Norma places her hand on David's back to guide him to the door. "Can you give us a second, please?" she asks. It is now time to douse Alexander's flame for Nyx. With the doppelganger on the way, the hunt for Charlie will soon begin. Norma is confident she will extract the intel needed—no matter how.

"He doesn't need to leave… David, stay!" Alexander insists that this is not the time. Norma insists that it is. Alexander battles the twofold insubordination—to his mother and to the true leader of Atropos. Which will effect a harsher scold? After what he just interrupted Alexander feels David could be an ally and maybe, just maybe this was *not* a time for defiance. This is an opportunity to rewrite the Atropos vow so that another vow can be made. A vow he so wishes to make as his seed grows until one day, before long, he or she sprouts as the newest branch in Veurr tree. The brilliant karats are hiding in his pockets eager to come out and shine a light into Norma's eyes that Nyx could never be nixed. That she and Alex have already altered the vows so many years ago. That, like Norma, defiance for irrational protocol runs deep in his veins also.

Alexander reaches into his coat pocket ready to obey, whether it be his mother or the Atropos director. He hopes his timing proves more favorable than David's. The beautiful turquoise box marked "Tiffany & Co." is revealed. Alexander sets it on top of the desk, then stands, waiting for the mother who spent her life protecting him from the agency.

Norma sits in the seat and returns her focus on Charlie and preparing for the awaited arrival of the doppelganger. “For a second I thought this was about the girl you’ve been warned to remove from your mind…” She pauses, then hopeful, she asks, “Did your father arrange this gift for me…? Put it away!”

“No,” Alexander says. Norma slowly turns her eyes to see him standing tall, firm. She looks to David as he steps to Alexander’s side. This ambush is much more than she can take. She reminds Alexander of his vow to Atropos. Alexander reminds her of her vows and how she’d defied the order.

“Alexander, that was different. There is a piece you are missing that your father and I had,” Norma says.

“How is my love for Nyx any different than the love you had for Father?” Alexander begins to anger. He will make her see the future that he so desperately wants, the future he so desperately will have.

“You! We had you. I left to protect you.”

“Yet here we are,” Alexander says.

“Norma. We can protect them. Nothing will happen. Let our boy have what his soul desires. We can change our paths now,” David pleas for Alexander. In return, he pleas for himself. Norma demands for it to end now.

“No, Mother, and there is no missing piece,” Alexander says. The room goes quiet.

The door handle turns and Donovan’s cane pushes, breaking the silence. He stops cold, feeling the tension in the room. “What the hell is going on here?” he asks.

Norma rises from her seat, reaches for the little turquoise box, grabs it, and then places it back inside Alexander’s coat pocket. Her hand softly strokes the side of his face, then she places her hand on his chest. She looks to David. He can see in her eyes anger, fear, love, warmth, with the idea that Alexander has all that she had ever wanted for him.

"What did I miss?" Donovan asks.

"Not now," Norma says. "We have a guest arriving soon." Norma leans down the chair in front of the desk and grabs her jacket, leaving Alexander, David, and Donovan to catch up.

CHAPTER 21

Norma steps into the abandoned warehouse, then stops as her mind vividly replays the scenes that happened the last time she was ever to hear or touch Alex's dying lips. It's dark and the only switch that is about to flip is within her. She can sense the light wane as she welcomes the darkness. Ever since she was a child, Norma has cautiously flipped the switch to fight the demons around her with hopes that humanity finds a way to turn back on. Alex always knew where to find it, and with a simple touch, lightness would shine from her eyes. Caution died with Alex on this floor. David follows closely behind her.

"I can do this," he says.

"No… this will be my pleasure."

Alexander hesitantly enters, looking at the floor to where his father had lay bleeding. He looks to Norma and notices his mother's methodical stare. He wonders if her choosing this site was sensible. The remaining Atropos would expect no less. Security surrounds the building to ensure no interruptions. The one over all agencies fed Norma with enough leeway to satiate her hunger.

Clank, clank sounds from Donovan's cane hitting the dirty concrete floor. He shuffles over trash while swatting larger scraps to the side to make his path to Norma.

"You do not need to be here," she says. Norma can see the pain over his face is not from the incessant pain he is in from a broken, missing bone. "Go back to the office and wait there. Get everything of help that Elizabeth shared and get it together. The clock is ticking for that little boy." Norma can see relief come across Donovan's face. He will not oppose.

Her guest has arrived. Xavier and the rest of the team drag him to the center of the room. The doppelganger's eyes have been blinded and his hand and feet are shackled. As Donovan crosses his path he swings his cane to swat what he sees as the biggest piece of trash out of his way. Norma nods to Xavier. The blindfold is ripped from the doppelganger's eyes for him to see what awaits him. She signals to the same scaffold where she, Alex, and Donovan had hung just months ago. Norma can sense his fear. She likes the smell.

"Wait. I have something for you," David says, turning to leave the building room.

Norma watches as the doppelganger is unlocked from the handcuffs only to be re-cuffed to the scaffold to hang. She walks to Alexander and whispers, "Leave. I don't want you here. Go home." Alexander knows this is without doubt not the time to challenge her. He begins to walk away but stops. He must know.

"Am I still Atropos?" he asks, anxious for her answer.

"*Donec mors nos separaverit*," she whispers (Until death separates us).

David returns passing Alexander as he leaves with a gift for their guest—more so for Norma. Alexander looks down at David's hand and smiles. In his hand is one of the two-sided Heretic Forks with collars; the same forks that were tightly strapped around Alex's and Donovan's necks. Now if his head moves he will experience the four sharp spines piercing into his neck. Two near the chin and two near the sternum. When Raiden collected it, David had ordered him to give it to him for safe keeping until such an occasion. Xavier straps the collar on tight.

"Fucking asshole! Who and where are those kids?" Xavier wastes no time. The doppelganger can feel the fiery spit as Xavier yells in his face. "Who are those kids?"

"Stand down," Norma yells.

"Xavier!" David yells louder.

Xavier reluctantly pulls back, charged, ready to be released. Norma will do the honor to extract what they need to find Charlie. Xavier will have his time deep within tunnels, hotels, or wherever the search takes them to bring the innocent home. Norma is coming to believe her profile of Xavier is correct. His hinges are typically tight despite his propensity for violence when a battle occurs. She is certain now that, like her, a few of his scars are from much younger days.

Norma circles the doppelganger. Her voice is calm. "What is your name?" she asks. He ignores her, then allows the forks to pierce his flesh as he turns his head down to spit in her face, attempting to defile. The effort proved inane. With a menacing smile, Norma wipes her face, then once again calmly repeats, "What is your name?" She will start with a name. It would be rude to begin without proper introduction. Besides, if she is to add to the haunting ghosts that whisper to her, she would at least like to know his name.

He rambles, speaking Dari. Norma recognizes his native tongue. In Latin, she calls for Lander and Stefen, whose fluency in Dari would make one think they were natural-born Afghans. Appearance, however: Lander, a self-proclaimed lion man, is obviously Swedish pedigree with his golden mane and pale skin. Stefen's Italian charisma could never be mistaken. David quietly joins them by their side.

"It's Afghan *tarana* (chanting): 'death in battle,'" Lander says.

"Fuck this!" Xavier takes the black scarf from his neck and shoves it in the man's mouth. His hand grabs the doppelganger's black wavy hair and pulls his head down until the forks tines bury deep into his flesh. "There, that's better. I can't listen to his jihadist propaganda bullshit anymore."

Norma grabs Xavier by the arm and pulls him away from the group. "Enough! You will have your time. Right now we need to find that boy, and the only way we're going to do that is if I can get it out of him how to find Charlie. Control your personal demons, Xavier." She releases his arm to return to where the doppelganger hangs, undaunted by his fate. Norma will have a better chance to retrieve the intel they need. She is confident that he will not allow her impure hands to take him from the pure hands of the seventy-two virgins that await him. In his world, to be killed by a woman is dishonorable. Norma pulls old trusty out from her back. She takes the knife and slides the tip down his chest, only cutting his shirt.

"Just the tip," she says, taunting that the rest of the blade will soon penetrate him. Norma shouts, grabbing and shaking his waist. "What is your name?"

His neck becomes taut, straining to keep his head straight. Blood is dripping down from his neck. For a second Norma feels his angst but quickly reminds herself that neither she nor any man in this room would ever kill or trap the innocent. He is not innocent. After all, he was responsible for Chris Logan and the guard that killed Alex. She begins to unzip his pants.

He spits the scarf out from his mouth. "Abdul," he yells out.

Norma stops. "There, that wasn't so hard now, was it? Well Abdul, my name is Norma." She stands before him twirling the knife around and around, taunting and persuading him to answer the next few questions she has prepared for him. She glances over to David as he stands with arms crossed ready to watch as Norma expertly plots her next move. "Who were those children at the hotel in Iraq? Where do you send them?" Norma takes out Charlie's picture and raises it to his face. "Have you seen this boy? Where is he?"

Silence is only broken by car horns blaring in heavy traffic, and the brakes of buses hissing through the broken windowpanes of the rundown industrial building.

Norma becomes agitated, annoyed that time is wasting on his intractable tongue. Abdul begins to chant, then emotions scream out in defiance. Xavier is beginning to become more restless. Norma scowls and grows even more impatient. "You look just like your father…You know, it only took one bullet to his head to save my son. How many bullets do you think it will it take to kill his?" Norma takes the Glock out from her waist and slides one in the chamber. Atropos stands awed by her cool reserve. “Maybe one for each one of the virgins I’ll save from your foul soul.” Norma looks around the room, then adds, “Wait, let’s see. How many bullets do we have here?” She begins to loudly count the men. “One, two, three, four…”

Xavier stops her. “Fuck this. This pig isn’t going to talk. Let me at him!” The scowl in Norma eyes warns him. David backs Norma up.

She continues until she reaches Milo. “Let’s see, nine, well ten, because I will make damn sure the bullet that ends your miserable life is the one from my chamber. I think we have seventy-two.” The men squirm as she resumes lowering his zipper with the tip of her knife. His pants drop to his ankles, stopping and snagging by the cuffs. “Don’t worry. I’m much nicer than the henchmen you sent. You know—” She pauses then points to the middle of the room where Chris Logan tried to befoul her “—it was there that your boy tried to savagely rape me. Of course, that was right before I cut his dick off and fed it to him.” Norma nods to Lander to come over. Xavier steps forward, but Norma quickly stops him with her extended arm. She again looks to Lander and nods once more. “How superficial can you get? We wouldn’t want our guest leaving us too soon.” As the other men move to the side, Lander takes a few steps back, then fires his gun. Abul grunts as the hot gilding metal grazes his leg. Norma steps back in front of Abdul. “I know that smarts, doesn’t it.” She sees the scars on his leg covering with blood. “I heard about how you got those scars. How many US soldiers did you kill that day?” she taunts. Abdul refuses the language that she could identify.

Stefen interprets Abdul's words and tells Norma that he will not give her what she wants. Old trusty doubts Abduls willingness to allow a woman to disgrace him. Norma has faith that old trusty is correct. She stabs the knife into the scarred leg and yanks it down, filleting his flesh. Her hand reaches up and his underwear drops on top of his pants exposing him. "I am going to ask you one more time. I am growing impatient. Who were those children at the hotel in Iraq? Where do you send them? Where is this boy?"

"You Americans are so righteous. Who do you think brings them to us? Who do you think buys them?" Abdul continues, this time using a language Norma can understand. "If I tell you, you will still kill me."

Norma stares deep into his eyes and vows to Abdul that if he talks, no harm will come to him by her hand. Perhaps a warrior code, perhaps trusting the Geneva Conventions will protect him in this warehouse, or just perhaps he can see that Norma is honorable and that by talking she would save him from a dishonorable death. Abdul believes her.

He tells her of tunnels within the US used to smuggle the children out and where to look. The prices fetched for a four-year-old little girl or boy. Like an Iraqi babbler, Abdul chatters the grizzly, horrific intel needed to start their mission to find Charlie and the other innocent missing, stolen children that have been or about to be sold into the child sex trade or organ harvesting. Norma sighs in despair and prays that they are not too late.

Norma places old trusty back into its sheath.

"Are you fucking serious?" Xavier yells. His brawny chest puffs breaths of vulgar fury that this was over. That this is all this merciless, vile monster would receive. “Norma! Are you fucking serious? You’re going to let this heartless motherfucker go?”

Norma turns her back and begins to leave. “I will never sacrifice my honor for this scum.” She takes a few steps and turns slightly. “Xavier,” she calls out. His growing disappointment deafens her words as raging eyes stare down Abdul. “Xavier,” she calls louder. He turns and sees her smile. “Send him to his seventy-two virgins.”

Norma leaves with David by her side. Atropos soon follows. Before any of them could pass under the burnt-out exit sign, a deafening bang rings their ears. Norma, David, and the Atropos men turn to see Xavier standing in front of Abdul’s dead body hanging with forks deeply embedded into his neck. His head is bowed down, his chest blown wide open. They watch as Xavier remains facing Abdul, fiddling with his body.

“Xavier let’s go,” Norma says.

He turns holding Abduls heart within his hand as blood drips from between his fingers. “See, I told ya’ll… Heartless motherfucker!”

Norma begins to walk out, shaking her head, expecting to hear Alexander’s jesting voice yell back to Xavier. *Who damaged you?* she hears clearly, then remembers he was not there.

CHAPTER 22

Alexander paces the floor, watching the grandfather clock hands tick the time closer until Nyx arrives. He looks at the clock, then his watch to assure himself the time is right. His eyes move back and forth, back and forth. Clock, watch, clock, watch, as his hand repeatedly reassures that the little turquoise box is safe inside his coat pocket. He takes a sip of water and places the glass onto the coffee table. *She's late,* he thinks. *I don't have much time before the hunt for Charlie begins. Mom is right, I need to fix this before we leave.* A sudden rush of doubt crosses his mind, then just as quickly vanishes. Nyx has long expressed her desire for a symbol, a license, something that moves their relationship status and eventually tie them together, forever. And now with the baby, he is sure she will be all too happy to say the word he's so eager to hear: yes. Nervous butterflies flutter in his stomach. His legs have weakened, his palms are sweaty, so he paces, waiting. *I miss you, Dad.* His heart aches, wishing for one of his wisdom talks to calm his nerves. He can feel his father's hand on his shoulder letting him know he is there. That he is proud, happy for his son and not to worry; all will be all right. That his love will prevail and that his happiness was all his mother ever wanted. "I hope you're right," he whispers into the air. *Mom did it, then eventually Dad, so why can't I have both, Atropos and Nyx. "Stop worrying, son."* He can hear the answer to his thoughts. *"Time will tell all."* He grabs the glass and chugs it down.

A light knock rushes Alexander to the door. "She's here." He quickly opens it, then stalls to see his deepest desires standing right in front of him. The butterflies are ready to take flight.

Nyx chuckles. "Alexander. What's gotten into you?" She jumps into his arms and playfully wraps her legs around his waist. Alexander carries her inside and kicks the door closed. She releases her legs and slides slowly down keeping her arms around his neck. "I missed you today," she says. She rises on the tips of her toes stealing a kiss. "So, Mr. Veurr. What's going on? What did you need to tell me?"

"You shouldn't be jumping like that," he says. He leans down and gently rubs her belly. "How's my boy?"

"Oh, Alexander, he's fine…Wait, boy? How do you know it's not a girl?" She laughs at Alexander's fuss and persistence to believe it is a boy. His hands continue to softly rub, then he cradles and kisses where he feels the baby to be. "And here I was worried about your mother being overly protective over you." Alexander lowers to his knee. His eyes rise to meet hers as his heart pounds, speaking to hers. Her soul offers him peace. "What's wrong?"

"I love you," he whispers.

Her smile whispers back, "I love you."

Alexander can see anything he could ever want is cradled within his hands. He can feel his father nudging him. Nyx reaches for his arms, then raises him. He can tell by the concern in her eyes that she sees his nervousness.

"Is everything okay?" she says, uncertain, as his energy rattles her calmness.

"No," he says.

Nyx begins to worry. "What! What's wrong?"

"I am struggling in vain here. This will not do…My feelings, my love for you will no longer be repressed." Alexander releases his soul free from its own self to blend with hers, to fuse to become one. His lips hunger to take a kiss, but that must wait. He continues. "Since the day those beautiful hazel eyes looked up at me, my heart had fallen afraid… Now I must say, without fear, I am irrevocably in love with you, Nyx." He takes her hands into his to hold. "With your slightest touch dark shadows leave my dreams. When we make love, then lie at night together, your warming breath blankets me, giving me comfort. I can no longer live my life with you like this. I am forever yours." Alexander reaches into his chest pocket. The little turquoise box that he has done well to safeguard opens. The flawless, exceedingly large diamond sparkles brilliantly. "Marry me."

Nyx gasps as her hand extends, shaking. "Yes," she cries. Alexander slips the ring onto her finger. She lunges into his arms weeping. She quotes from a love letter Beethoven had written to his one true love, "Ever thine, ever mine, ever ours." Alexander finally steals his kiss. He then leans down for another kiss for his baby "boy," excited to tell him she said yes. He can feel his father's arm wrap him with pride.

"Let's celebrate," Nyx says.

"I can't. I hate to bring this up now. We're heading out tonight." Alexander commits completely. "We need to talk about what I do. You may change your mind after I tell you. Why we leave abruptly. Why I'm wounded at times."

Nyx eyes look down to her adorned finger rocking the diamond to flicker. She is certain that nothing he can say will take this ring off her finger. Her trust, her belief in him could never be wrong. "I don't care what you do. I know your heart and know whatever you do is for good." Her worry is the one question she knows must be asked. "Does your mother know? Have you told her?"

That felt more complicated to Alexander than explaining Atropos. "I showed her the box. I believe that was clear."

"Did you tell her I'm pregnant?"

"I was in the middle of telling her when we were interrupted… She and I will be working together on this trip. I will tell her then."

"Are you sure you shouldn't have waited?"

Alexander ponders the question for a second, then insists that he could not wait for his return. He knows his return is never guaranteed. "This I am sure. My mother has always wished for this life for me. She left when I was born to give me this life. I know my father will speak to her. Time will tell all. She would never stand in the way of my happiness."

The door knocks rapidly alerting that someone needs to see Alexander immediately. Alexander and Nyx look hesitant as to who that may be. *Bam* pounds the door. A strong guess comes to Alexander as he slowly goes to the door to open it.

"The doppelganger gave us the intel we needed to find Charlie. Let's move out," Norma says, slipping between Alexander and the door.

"Time to go, son," David says, following Norma closely.

Norma and David abruptly stop, watching as Nyx quickly hides her hand behind her back. "Oh, you have company," Norma says.

"I was just leaving," Nyx says, speeding toward the door.

"Stop," Norma yells out. "Please come back here." Nyx, no matter that she is not Atropos, obeys Norma's commanding voice. David whispers in Norma's ear to move with ease. He reminds her to think of Alex. Norma shrugs him out of her ear. Alexander steps in front of Nyx, shielding her from Norma's pending words. "You have become an important part of my son's life. Do you feel the same? Do you love him?" It appears that Norma's interrogation tactics have resumed. Norma feels Alex's soft touch and sees his tender eyes, calming what he thinks is a storm that is brewing. How the thought of him calms her to reason is remarkable. How she longs to feel his presence is cruel.

"Mother," Alexander warns. He positions himself in front of Nyx. Her petite body is protected behind his six-foot shield. "We will talk later." Nyx comes out from behind Alexander and moves to his side. She grabs his hand to hold.

"Definitely, yes," she says. Her eyes are soft but her love is firm. She looks to Alexander. He smiles as he looks back to her. "He is my everything." Nyx stands fearless facing Norma. "Yes, I love him!"

Norma spots the ring on Nyx's finger at the same time David catches sight of it. Alexander can feel Norma's stare peer deep into his soul. David steps to stand beside Alexander. Norma looks as the three look back at her waiting, ready to defend.

"Is this what you two want?" Norma asks. She looks to Alexander. "Are you ready to give up everything for her?'

"Definitely, yes," he says.

Norma replays the day she and Alex stood hand in hand as she vowed never to return to the agency. Norma steps to face Alexander. She locks her eyes onto him, then unexpectedly turns to Nyx. Norma looks deep into Nyx's eyes. "Are you ready to give up everything for him?" Nyx smiles wholeheartedly, then nods. Norma raises her hand and places it gently on Nyx's face. She brushes back an auburn lock that has fallen in her face. "So be it," she says. Three sets of lungs expel breaths that were held in anticipation. "Welcome to the family, Mrs. Veurr."

Nyx elbows Alexander. Alexander hesitates, catching his breath. Nyx takes the lead. She reaches for Norma's hand. She places it on her belly. Norma quickly pulls it away and jerks back. Norma looks to Alexander, then back to Nyx. She looks to David. David smiles as happiness for them shows. Nyx grabs Norma's hand and places it again on her belly. This time Norma feels as her bloodline beats inside Nyx's womb. Norma's face drops and the wells of her eyes begin to fill. She holds her hand firmly against Nyx's stomach, switching back and forth from looking to her stomach to, surprisingly, looking at Nyx.

"Congratulations, Grandma," Nyx says. Her face glows, radiating the love she already has for the life that is growing within her. "Alexander has said you would always protect him. Now you will have another. I need you with us," she says.

"*Donec mors nos separaverit*," she whispers.

David grabs Norma in for a tight hug. "Congratulations, Grandma," he says, kidding that the rites of passage has come to call. Alexander takes his turn to embrace his mother closely. He whispers, "Thank you," then whispers again, "Thanks, Dad."

"If we don't have any more surprises, we need to go. Everyone will be waiting soon to head out," Norma says. As Norma and David move toward the door, she stops as Alexander rushes to get ready. "Alexander, you can sit this one out," she says.

Alexander replies, "Is that an order?"

"Only if you want it to be," Norma says as she and David walk out the door.

"I'm coming. We're going to find Charlie. I'll meet you at The World Renaissance," Alexander yells just as the door shuts.

Nyx watches as Alexander prepares. She is getting an understanding that her soon to be husband is government and no doubt secret. She feels safe knowing he is capable of defending. "When will you be back?"

"I never know," he sighs. He stuffs clothes into his bag, then grabs his gun and wallet off the coffee table. Everything else will be waiting for him at The World Renaissance. "You remember how to lock up?" he asks. Alexander takes a minute to show Nyx all that is important. He kisses her and begins to leave. As the door begins to close, he suddenly reopens it as if something has nearly been forgotten. He drops his bag and grabs Nyx. "I love you," he says. He passionately kisses her, then takes one more kiss for the baby. "See you soon, lil man," he says.

CHAPTER 23

As they stand huddled, ready to go underground at The World Renaissance Hotel, an unfamiliar outsider walks up with Norma, Alexander, David, and Donovan. They can tell by the jeans, dark long-sleeve tunic, boots, and full face mask pulled down around his neck that he must be Special Ops. His presence here in front of them tells them he must be agency approved. Alexander spots that his watch is inverted. Only a skilled cell hunter would know to turn his watch backward so the crystal face of the watch would not reflect sunlight, giving away detection. Alexander then startles, noticing that his mother is dressed and preparing for the mission ahead. She is blacked out, wearing her standard form-fitting pants, shirt, and jacket. They were unusually dressed to blend in as civilians. The usual black attire was rolled tightly in bags.

"Are you really joining us?" Alexander asks.

"Yes," Norma says. She drops the black rucksack to the floor and verifies that everything she will need is accessible as Donovan makes the introduction.

"Team, this is Craig. He used to be Delta Force and is now the leading expert on human trafficking cartels. He will be a huge asset, so listen up," Donovan says.

"I have spent the last eight years busting up human trafficking operations from all over the world—Columbia, Haiti, Philippines, Kenya, China, India, Mexico...This year alone we have liberated two thousand and nine children. In that number were children sold here within the United States. There are some prominent names, hotels, and online shopping companies that are suspected to be part of these operations. They find a SKU number online in the kids' section with a child pictured in an ad, then go to the dark website and put that number in. The type of child that was chosen in the ad is then purchased. It is just one of the ways these children are sold in the sex trafficking industry. Gentlemen, slavery is alive and well in the land of the free. It is a multi-billion-dollar industry. This will not be like anything you are used to. Two months ago in Tucson we found two cells. In one cell the children were shoved through trapdoors behind a wall and closed up but for small slot at the bottom of the sheetrock that could be opened, then closed. Food and water were thrown at them until a buyer came to take them to their final hell. The other we stumbled on was an underground bunker with solar lights. It was five feet tall, and inside we found crates large enough to fit a child, a crib, hair dye, a cot, and pornographic material. Outside... there were three trees with hand and leg restraints wrapped around... Just a couple days later we intercepted a group of children in California being trafficked. They had been transported underground through a tunnel out of Mexico. We caught them blocks from it. These men."

Xavier interrupts, clearly angered. "We already know about these sick motherfuckers. Tell us how we can kill them." Xavier is ready to make Craig's number rise to two thousand and ten.

"You're going to have to use your trained eye to look for signs outside of the obvious. Like I said, listen to the walls. They will talk to you if you listen. Donovan has briefed me of your mission and the intel about the child you are looking for. The terrorist cell that is linked to this case we had been tracking. Terrorists have been funded for a long time on the billions made from trafficking these poor children. Sadly, they are not the only ones…Norma has found a backdoor by using the link to Chris Logan. The hotel on your first stop will be a good starting point with sightings of him there…Keep in mind that underground bunker in Arizona had been vacated just two days before we got there, so timing will be crucial." Craig continues to condense his eight years of findings into twenty minutes. He tells them of a recent cell bust in California only days prior and the children recovered. He reminds them that Charlie has been missing for five days now and the window that is closing in on them. Before turning to leave, he offers one more thing. "Whatever you stumble on we will be behind you to help bring these kids home. Good luck, men." The Atropos team watches Craig head down the hallway, then disappear as he exits through the secret door.

Xavier continues to loudly express his blood thirst for the thieves of innocence. Alexander and David take the lead through the underground tunnel that will take Atropos to the helipad where their transportation awaits. Norma stalls for a quick word with Donovan.

"Are you sure you need to go?" Donovan asks. "No one would blame you for standing down on this one. You need more time to get your head clear of Alex's ghost. His death about killed you."

"You are starting to sound like Alexander and David. I wish you all would stop telling me what I need. You're forgetting that I created this team. I trained them. I'm going to find that boy!" Norma reaches down for the rucksack. She tosses it over her shoulder, then pauses to look Donovan in the eye. "Don't worry, old man. You're old, crippled ass will beat me to the pearly gates."

"At least wear Kevlar," Donovan nags of over two and a half decades of her determined habit to remain light. He raises the Kevlar vest that he had been carrying, urging her to take it.

Norma smiles and lightly pats Donovan on the back. "Tell Elizabeth I'll be bringing her boy home soon." She turns and walks off, leaving the Kevlar in Donovan's hand.

The idle pilot watches Norma as she nears. The blades begin to spin rapid gusts of wind. Norma approaches David and Alexander standing outside of the helicopter with their heads down. The remaining Atropos is loaded and rearing to go. "Do we have everything? Weapons and equipment loaded?" she asks.

"This helicopter is full. There's only room for ten," David says.

"Go home, Mom," Alexander says.

First Donovan, now them, too. Norma is becoming annoyed and stubborn to reason. "I'm fine. You will need me on this mission. Remember, these kids are going to be frightened from the hellish nightmare they are in. You will need me to calm them, to gain their trust."

"Are you sure?" David asks, then reminds her that it was only recently that her eyes were closed, seeing Alex. By now David should know that it doesn't take a fallen lid to see Alex.

"Is this what this is about, David?"

"Of course not," David says.

"Mom, nobody expects you to do this."

"Did you not lose a father? Yet has anyone questioned your ability to lead this team?"

"Mom, it's different. If I lost Nyx..."

"Enough," Norma says. She motions for them to board and to end such absurd nonsense. David hops in, then Alexander. Norma jumps on, then looks back as Atropos men are quietly sitting, staring at her. David was right. This helicopter was full... of the highest regard. Xavier stands and roars loudly as the pilot throttles the blades to chop the cold air in whisper mode. Lander, Kosmo, Stefen, and Vali root louder as Milo, Nick, and Raiden are soon to follow. Alexander and David sit looking at one another, shrugging whether this is truly a good idea. Norma sits near the pilot, then replaces the men's loud clamor with Bach's *Well-Tempered Clavier* beautifully playing in her ears.

CHAPTER 24

Atropos lands on the hotel's rooftop, then moves quickly to the door that takes them to the top floor. With Norma in the lead, closely they follow one by one, careful of cameras, guests, and hotel staff. A middle-aged man, average height and largely round, dressed in a fine tailored business suit, comes out from a room. Norma halts them. She waits, peeking, as he ushers a much younger scantily dressed female, sixteen at most, to the elevator doors. His hand nudges her back to enter the elevator. Norma listens for the two metal panels to slide together, closed. She signals to fall back to the rooftop.

"David, you come with me. The rest stay here near the helicopter."

"What about me?" Alexander says. He looks to David with anxious eyes. Norma being the true leader he must obey. With one tap of the finger Alexander is linked to Norma and David to spy their every move. Their voices will speak back to him if a threat discovers them.

"Just be ready," Norma says. She throws her rucksack to Xavier. Her black jacket is removed, then she pulls out her shirt to cover the gun that is tucked into her tightly fit waistband. Norma removes the hair band that tightly bound her tresses to allow them to fall. Her head shakes, waving her raven hair free. She tosses her jacket to Xavier.

"What am I, your butler?" he jokes. Xavier gets a faint scent of lavender. He raises her jacket to his nose and inhales deeply. "Ahhhh. Fresh as a summer breeze." Alexander lightly punches Xavier in the chest.

"Can't you ever be serious? Fuck-head!" Alexander demands focus.

"Does Nyxie let you kiss her with that mouth? I'll seriously kick that little ass I used to wipe," Xavier says.

"Enough," David warns. David looks to Norma to see her slight grin. It is during these missions when bonds form that withstand time. David takes cue and removes his pullover jacket, un-tucks his shirt over his gun to hang over his jeans, then replaces his cap.

"Let's go, hubby," she says.

If only, he thinks.

Norma and David amble through the door pretending to hold a key to one of the posh rooms. The hotel's famous H crest is emblazoned on the walls. Norma mumbles, "You would never think a hotel of this caliber would be accused of turning a blind eye, much less hosting such atrocities."

They reach the elevator door, and Norma presses the button just as the elevator opens. It's the same man seen earlier, only this time he is ushering a different scantily dressed, much younger female. This one is maybe thirteen. Norma sickens as forged words leave her lips. "Good evening," she says. She entices the girl for eye contact. "That is a beautiful dress you are wearing. Where did you get that?" The girl timidly responds, thanking her, as the man rejects Norma's ploy for honeyed chat. Norma watches as they walk down the hallway. When they stop at the door, the younger female turns her head, looking back to Norma as the man scans the key card. He shoves her inside. "I think we are in the right spot," Norma says, hitting the exclusive staff button.

Using the intel given, Norma and David find their way into the basement, where hotel sheets, blankets, and towels agitate in washers and twirl to dry. The washing machines and dryers drown their footsteps. It will be hard to detect little voices. She can recall Craig saying, "If you listen, the walls will talk." David pulls a thermal gun from his waist as Norma pulls a gun. She loads the chamber, ready for whatever they might find or whoever may find them. The gun beams across the wall two feet from the floor. It's certain that it'll find even the smallest of trapped souls.

"What are you two doing in here?" a voice calls, startling them. Norma hides behind David's back as the man looking to be barely in his twenties appears indifferent to them, nevertheless tending to finishing dryer and wash cycles. His slick hair hangs to his shoulders, and the uniform looks to have missed its wrinkle-free cycle. Norma comes out from behind David's back, pulling on her sports bra. She then pulls the shirt quickly back down. She fakes embarrassment. David joins in.

"I'm sorry, man. My wife and I were just having some fun." David gazes over to Norma. "Wow, 'my wife.' I love the sound of that." Norma leans in and plants a passionate kiss. "We were just married and spending our honeymoon here," David says. He kisses her, then looks back to him. "I wanted to show her I can be adventurous," David says. Norma and David sense it to be working by the uncomforted yet baked look on his face. The young man smiles as his flighty eyes look to be giving David an air high-five. David looks at the guy's name pinned on his chest. It reads: JOSHUA. Shaggy would be more fitting.

"You got five minutes. I'll be sure no one disturbs ya," he says. He's slow to leave the room as five minutes to him will most likely time lapse to five hours.

"Really," David says as they quickly resume searching for the intel's accuracy. Norma signals to Alexander that they are coming up empty. They begin to walk out the door when Norma stops. There is an unusual break in the wall, calling attention to her. Not quite the voice she expected to hear. She had assumed when Craig said listen to the walls, he meant for children's voices not her own warning to suspicious clues. David slides his hand, pressing against the ridge of the panel. Norma was spot on. The wall opens to steps leading underground. They enter and turn to close the door. David's certain when the young man returns he will question the weed he had puffed just before his shift. It must have been laced with "some good shit," as he imagines the stoner might say, as he doubts ever seeing them there.

Norma brings the watch closer to her mouth to tell Alexander they found something and how to find it. "Follow my coordinates," she says. She instructs them to travel light and two by two and be aware of the young hotel staff on laundry duty. This was not to be a shock combat tactic, although she doubts there could be anything that could shock that kid right now. It has been deemed needless to this point. Norma and David wait for the team to join them. David teases her to the skit so well performed and to how acting wasn't what made it believable.

"Wifey."

Norma sees that once this is all over, he will be relentless.

The wall slides, then Alexander and Xavier enter. It is not long before the rest take the steps down to where they wait. The mustiness of the earthen walls is pungent as is the soiled air that flows through this dark tunnel. Xavier leans into Norma and sniffs.

"That's better," he comments at the faint scent of lavender. "Any idea where this goes?" Xavier asks.

Guns are retrieved from waistbands while others raise legs of jeans to pull weapons from their boots. Noise suppressors are attached. "Here." Xavier tosses one to her, then a headset that is set to uncover the blanket that would darken their eyes. Norma tightens it onto her gun, thermal goggles strap on, then she adjusts old trusty to a more comfortable position on her back.

"Let's go." Norma gestures to move deeper into this mysterious tunnel with green, yellow, and red images guiding them as Donovan's voice joins them in their ear. In two lines they follow closely behind Norma and David with senses fully alert and a hand on the shoulder in front of them.

"Is this whole country built on top of fucking tunnels," Alexander whispers to Xavier.

"Looks like it," Xavier says.

Norma wearily glances back to Alexander, warning that little ears may be around him soon. Alexander looks to his mother, certain that he and David are right. She should not have joined them. Norma has looked weary since the day his father died and even more so learning of child sex trafficking and harvesting. Maybe now she will retire her aged combat boots. Alexander hopes.

David's arm spans right across, telling Norma to stop as guns point in the air. Ears listen intently to understand the noise that they hear. It is impossible. The muffled voices are too distant. They wait and listen. Norma touches David's hand for them to move. The rocky walls scratch their sides as they pass by. Eleven boots slowly move five hundred feet until a distant dim light comes to view. Tiny pitches sniffling, whimpering is clear as the larger, fuming voices scold for silence.

Atropos counts the different tones. They hear one, two, three, four deep, gravelly tones. They will need to move quickly. At any time someone could join them from behind. Norma removes old trusty from its sheath, readying it for duty. "We need to be precise, Xavier," Norma warns. "There are children in there. Make it quick, make it stick." Norma advances.

The Atropos team swarms in as Norma runs to the first cage, then another, then another, calling Charlie's name. Three white, bearded but bald men shock with frozen eyes as their warm, stout bodies fall dead to the ground. Not one of their guns discharged. The chambers lay full next to them. The fourth man charges Milo with a knife. Milo sweeps his leg, kicking the man in the knee, not quite throwing him off balance. The man lunges at Milo, slicing his arm. Xavier charges, grabbing the man by his hair and flipping him back.

He takes his knife and stabs the man in the chest. His hand hammers, driving the knife into the man's heart, certain to stop it from beating.

"This is why you don't play with your food," he whispers to Milo as he examines Milo's wound. Xavier tosses him a roll of gauze to wrap it, then heads to the cages.

The initial threat has been executed.

"Charlie," Norma calls out, searching cages one by one. "Charlie?"

Atropos stands aghast, taking in the scene that surrounds them and the stench of urine and feces that violate their noses. Seductive dresses for the older girls, sundresses for the young, boy pants of all sizes, and oxfords, all hung on the portable rack. *H* is branded all over the hotel's complimentary items taken from the rooms. Food from the breakfast buffet still lies on the dirt floor outside of the cages. They are finally coming to understand to what depths this mission will take them. They spy around each cage filled with crimpled children shaking with fear. The kids are bruised, some beaten, others ripped beyond pain. They see white, black, brown faces that range from five to sixteen years old, looking back at them, terrified, wondering whether this is a rescue or a transfer to the next high bidder. The older girls and boys are hugging the younger ones, trying to ease their fear and quiet their cries. Norma gets to the last cage with no answer to her calls. She removes the key from one of the dead bodies, then opens the lock to help them out. Their legs have stiffened, faces dirty, eyes hungry for it to be all over. A little girl is the last to crawl out. Norma reaches down and lifts her up.

"You're safe now," Norma says. Alexander, David, Xavier are helped by Milo, Vali, and Kosmo as Lander, Stefen, Nick, and Raiden protect their backs. Xavier reaches down to help a little boy to his feet. The boy screams as panic strikes. Xavier wraps him in his arms, but the boy wails.

"Kill me. Please…No more," he cries, choosing death to stop his pain.

Norma rushes to Xavier and takes the boy from his arms. She softly shushes him, placing his head on her shoulder. The tenderness in her voice tells him: "No one will hurt you ever again." His innocence is forever lost by the apparent blood stains on the seat of his pants. Xavier spots it and rage that has been caged erupts. Xavier finds a metal bar and goes to one of the dead men. Norma stops him as Xavier begins to lower the dead man's pants.

"He's dead. The children," she says. The bar slams hard to the ground.

The little boy chokes on his tears, trying to catch his breath. "Ssssshhh." Norma completely removes the goggles, then passes them to David. She sings a sweet lullaby just as she had so many times before, chasing the boogeyman out from Alexander's nightmares. She peels him back for him to look at her. "You see that big scary guy right there?" Norma points to Xavier. "He's really a soft teddy bear. I promise you. He is my friend and is here to protect you. If he doesn't do what you say… you just tell me and I'll kick his butt. Do you trust me?" He gives her a little promising nod. "Can he hold you while I call for the other men that will help get you out of here?"

A little nod, then Norma hands Xavier the little boy. "We need to get them out of here before we have company." Norma calls for the older children's help. "Have you seen this boy?" She flashes a picture of Charlie. The girls shake their heads no. "Do you know where this tunnel leads?" she asks. They tell her tales of two paths they have or seen taken. One into the hotel lobby, where they are escorted to rooms to shower, then please the guests, only to return to cages until the next time, and one farther down that will lead them to a house that once traveled, they are never to return. It is in that house the final bid, bids them farewell—forever.

"I know this is hard, but I need to know everything so we can get you out of here." The girls tell Norma everything they can gather, in shame. They are uncertain as to who, how many, or the layout of the house. When they arrived in the middle of the night, they were drugged and blindfolded.

"I need you girls to do me a favor. Can you do it?" Norma asks. She entices for them to dig deep within this tunnel to find bravery. "I need your help with the smaller ones. They will trust you. When we walk down this tunnel, it will get dark. Can you keep them quiet?" They all gesture yes. "I'm proud of you girls." Norma offers them the first kind touch since being ripped of their virtue. One by one, they hug Norma.

Norma calls for Craig, eager for an answer. How long will it take for them to get to their coordinates? It was discussed that they were scattered across the US and a team would be near the hotel on standby. By the east direction she knew where the hidden passageway to be and the probable feet it will take to reach the house. She guides Craig to where he and his team will find them. Craig reassures her that his team is nearby and will penetrate quickly. "How many?" he asks.

Norma tells him twenty-eight. He advises to hold tight, fearful of children getting caught in the line of fire. Norma is sure he is right. She tells him they will take whatever comes their way but will give them the honor to do what they so desire to bring the house down.

A half hour passes. Norma, Alexander, David, and Donovan agree it's best to start moving through the dark path, allowing the walls to be their guide. They will shield the lead until steps confirm they are at the end of the tunnel. "Okay, kids," Norma calls out. "You are all honoree members of my team… We found you because you're brave, strong, and didn't let those bad people win. Now I need you to help me protect my men here. Will you help me?" Quietness will not come easy. These children will grow to always fear bumps in the night.

"I will," the teen girls speak up. "I will," continues from little voices trying to be heard.

Atropos moves the children through the darkness choosing to use cell phones and small luminescent flashlights to ease the kids' anxiety. It is eerily quiet, air stagnant, as the kids move closely behind. Minutes feel to be hours. They stop seeing steps that lead up to a passageway. Light is escaping through cracks of the wooden planks of the trap door. They're certain they have arrived and are standing under the house's floor. They are uncertain if it will be found or who will join them at the bottom of the steps. Trust of Craig and his team's skills are fading. Norma begins plotting their next move. Some of the Atropos men will follow her up the steps while others remain with the children. She raises her finger to her lips and presses against them, sure they have seen their teachers do this so many times before. Atropos steps the kids back away from the steps and motions for them to sit closely together, still and quiet as mice. For the kids time feels to be as motionless as they are. Scuffling can be heard above. Shots ring out. Atropos positions for whoever opens the door then comes down those steps. Guns are drawn, pointing to the stairs.

The hinges squeak. Legs come down first. Norma sighs, recognizing the boots, then pants, then face. He had been behind them the whole way, ensuring the cleanup wasn't left to one of the newest recruits.

"Come on, kids. It's time to go home," Craig says. He pats Norma on the back. "We will take it from here."

"I saw more in the hotel. Make a visit to the top floor."

"Well done," he says.

Not quite yet, Norma thinks.

CHAPTER 25

"What the hell are we in for?" David asks. Norma joins the Atropos team in the helicopter, ready for takeoff. It is unusually void of noxious air. Heads are down and eyes are solemn. Their next stop will be at a different hotel; only this time they will be key holders. Donovan has called ahead reserving the six rooms at the Grand Lux Hotel in Tijuana, Baja California. It was chosen for the location and helipad beside the hotel.

Atropos persists to keep moving. Time is flying faster than this stealth helicopter. Donovan insists for more time to process uploaded visuals, then searches the dark web for matches, giving confidence that at the end of the next suspected tunnel, they'll find Charlie. Being wrong would waste precious time and could prove fatal. He cannot rely on alleged traffickers slithering underground into Mexico. He needs to be definite that the previous bust has not compromised the tunnel and that it still flows free with frightened kids being shoved to and from as other children pass by happily, gripping their parents' hands for the promise of a new life. The intel has not been confirmed. While they wait, it has been ordered that they must break and reload.

Xavier looks around at the downtrodden faces. He shares their torment. The impact of those children is apparent. He sees Alexander staring out the window as the rotors rev. He searches deep to find his usual scepter against the travails of their missions. "You be the little spoon," Xavier says, hitting Alexander in the chest.

Alexander breaks free from the thoughts that are weighing profoundly on his mind. "There is no way I am sleeping next to your lumberjack, hairy ass. Why don't you take time to shave and stop scaring the hell out of these poor kids?" Alexander says.

"You wish you could grow a man's beard. What's that little shadowy goatee you're growing?" Xavier reaches to touch Alexander's face. Alexander ducks. "I had more hair on my nuts by the time I hit puberty… Wait, you're growing it for Nyxie, aren't you? Trying to make her think you're a man? Do I need to stop by and show her what a man really is?"

"Xavier, why are you such a douche?" Alexander laughs.

"Alexander and Nyx sittin' in a tree, k-i-s-s-i-n-g. First comes love, then comes…" Xavier makes a dramatic pause. "Oops."

Alexander quickly looks to Norma and David. Information travels faster in this team than a damn BOLO (be on the lookout) wire from the CIA. Norma grins.

"You're gonna name him Xavier, after me, aren't ya?"

"You'll never go around my child." Alexander muses on the idea of Xavier's tendency for profane outbursts, lack of patience. "I still can't believe Mom ever let you influence me as a kid. Now fucking look at me." There is not a soul, perished or present, that isn't aware of the fondness that Norma holds for this original Atropos.

"Xavier Junior. I like the sound of that." The banter stabs, then jabs quicker in the helicopter than the field in combat. The guys take turns slaying Xavier until Norma grows tired.

"Enough," she yells. She is aware this is how they survive. She is also aware that it's coming at her expense. Mozart is the only voice she wishes to hear. She needs to stop her heart from draining her mind of its vital purpose.

They land and begin to gear down. Shirts are loosened to cover tucked guns in order to blend. Rifles, spare cartridges, headsets, goggles, rucksacks bulging with arsenals, and utility belts will all remain on the helicopter until further orders. An agency keeper boards the helicopter. He appears as elusive as the men he serves.

"Good evening, gentlemen. These will be your keycards for your rooms. A change of attire and requested necessities will be waiting for you in your rooms. It is 12:01 PM. Move out is scheduled in less than four hours. Rest while you can. Have a good night." Short, to the point, and devoid of the concierge charm other guests will be given. Still it is five stars over the two long winks they typically get somewhere on a rainy mountain, hot desert, or swampy grassland. Before they enter, Norma must advise.

"Listen up, men. You heard him. We have four hours. Take this time to prepare for what lies ahead. As you saw in those children's eyes this will be more daunting than ambushing a terrorist camp under the cloak of night. We will need to be conscious of each bullet. Never before has 'make it quick, make it stick' rang more true."

Norma is first to jump down, then David, then Alexander, then the rest follow. As they begin to enter the hotel lobby, they scatter, acting as if strangers. Norma and David enter the elevator first as Alexander and Xavier choose steps to take them to the next floor. The rest walk alone in search of elevators or steps to take them to their assigned rooms. One room per floor they stack, with Norma ready to rest above them.

"After you shower, go find Alexander and come to my room. Donovan will brief us there." The elevator doors open and David steps out. He stalls to turn around. His eyes connect to Norma. The doors close breaking his hold. Norma sighs.

A tap on the door and Alexander answers.

"Are you ready?" David asks.

"Let me get my room key." Alexander turns as David follows him in. Xavier appears from the bathroom wearing only his lucky boxer briefs with elastic that is burdened around his waist.

"Lookey, it's a threesome. Not what I had in mind… Oh, what the hell," Xavier says. He begins to drop his boxers. David chuckles as Alexander pushes Xavier back into the bathroom. Xavier's bare feet slap the marble tiles as he tries to gain balance.

"Why am I being punished? He sounds like Bigfoot in there." Alexander laughs. He sits on the plush bed to put on socks, then boots.

"Your mom awaits," David says.

Xavier returns, this time in jeans with the top unbuttoned and no shirt. His back muscles flex as he reaches to the bed for the T-shirt he had chosen before leaving DC. He will dress, then rest ready.

David spies every scar on Xavier's body, replaying when each mark was made—except for one, the long scar crossing his back. He has seen it since they started Atropos together. "Are you ever going to tell me how you got that?" David asks. Xavier is quick to cover up. His silence once again speaks loudly that he will never answer. David, feeling to already have it, follows Alexander out the door.

Alex and David stand in Norma's room. She walks to the window. Her hand releases the tiebacks and rich red drapes fall together. "Donovan is on standby," Norma says. They walk to the bed, then sink into the comforter around the laptop with Donovan's hologram face floating in the air. They understand that time is vital, so they listen intently.

"With the images uploaded from the team's optic eye, there is a match to the last known picture found of Charlie. It was used in an auction we intercepted through a back channel to the dark web they use. The cages, dirt floor and walls, down to the branded items found, were put through computer forensics and prove to be the same as in this picture we intercepted. Charlie has been there. By checking the breakfast menu for each day and comparing it with the food on the ground in the picture of Charlie…I believe only two days before." Norma frustrates at the missed opportunity. She wonders if it's possible the older girls were in rooms of horror when Charlie passed by. When returned, their eyes were too sodden to notice. She didn't think to ask the younger children. It is a mistake certain not to be made again. "I think we're close," Donovan says. His hologram head bends, and the sound of a Zippo lighter sliding across the desk can be heard. Unconsciously, Norma's skin crawls as the Zippo does. An unexpected reaction. She refocuses, forcing Mackenzie out of her mind. This mission may prove harder than she believed, feeling more than Alex's ghost present. "As of now, the tunnel at these coordinates is still open for business. Craig will confirm," Donovan says.

All that has been discovered, all that has been pieced together was presented before them. Chris Logan had been sighted here, making this spot the next logical place to search. In less than three hours they will resume to learn how close they really are or if the missed opportunity proves that Charlie is lost forever.

Norma closes the laptop. "Get some rest now," she says.

"Alexander, go ahead. I need a minute with your mom," David says. David watches as the door closes. "Are you okay?" He can see the strain in her eyes.

"I'm fine," she says. She sees his desire to pick up from when they were interrupted. She begins to frustrate even more. "Go get some rest," she says, gesturing for him to go, to leave her now. David is quick to correct her. This was definitely not the time or his desire. He has waited over two and a half decades; he will wait until they're back in DC and Charlie is safely snuggled in his mother's calming arms. That is his intention. He stands and turns to walk away.

"David. Wait." She suddenly wants—needs—to feel his strength envelop her. Physical intimacy was not her craving.

She was hungry for an emotional touch. David turns around with tensing eyes. All their years together soon play back to her. In a second, she can see him evolve from a boyish heart to the deepened man that stands before her eyes. It is her that has resumed from when they were interrupted. She can feel Alex and hear his whispers telling her to allow David to fulfill a pact: let his love mend her broken soul. David's love has never been unrequited. It was just different.

David slowly walks to her. He grabs her hands and pulls her closer. His arms wrap her. Norma can feel his warm blood pumping. Tension releases, allowing the moment. "Do you want me to stay?" he asks.

"For a little," she says. Norma guides David to the bed. She sinks down into the lush plumes, lying on her back. David lies on his side facing her. His hand softly brushes her hair, cheek, then neck. Norma lies staring at the ceiling. "We have to find that boy. Not lie in here," she says. He leans in and his lips stroke her cheek. "We will," he whispers. Her eyes close and the light fades, her breath becomes shallow, and soon she hears the sounds of silence. For now he is content to be her medium. David watches as Norma drifts to Alex. It is him she truly needs.

CHAPTER 26

Norma's cell phone rings, startling her awake. "Mom, open up," Alexander says. Norma jumps up in the same mucky clothes he left her in. She glances at the amber numbers glowing 04:01 as she makes her way to the door. It's only been three hours since he left this room.

"I can't believe I beat you out," Alexander says. He looks at her disheveled hair. "Whoa, rough night?" David joins Norma's side. Shock drops Alexander's mouth open. Norma uses her finger to close his mouth, then disappears into the bathroom to steal a second to change clothes and prepare.

"It's not what you think," David says. Alexander returns to his duly noted support. David and Norma are unconcerned as to what Alexander thinks. "Is the team ready?" David asks. Alexander confirms all three S's have been accomplished—shit, shower, and shaved. Except for Xavier…he shaves for no one. All equipment and weapons are loaded and ready.

Within minutes Norma opens the bathroom door and rejoins them, fully dressed. Her oily hair is slicked, then bound in a tight bun. The only water to touch her body was a splash against her face to wake. She gears up as she stands by David's side. She adjusts old trusty, then laces her boots. The Glock gets tucked firmly into her waistband. It is a routine that muscle memory needs little coaching from her weary brain.

"Let's go," Norma says. Her key is left on the nightstand. They will not be returning. The keeper will wipe any trace that they were ever there. "I have one stop before we enter that tunnel." They choose the steps for less interruption of elevator stops and guests' nosy ears. "Donovan mentioned about the cell bust a couple days ago near the tunnel we will be entering. How one of the older children had been held captive for years. I had him set me up for a visit to where the girl is being treated… With the information Donovan provided, it may help us."

CHAPTER 27

Norma, at the side of the clinic doctor, steps up to the nurses' station. Her loathing for unclean messiness runs freely while cages and locked doors contain committed patients. If her daughter were in this facility, this would not be acceptable. By the overly stressed expressions on their faces, those working here appear soon to be patients at this mental health hospital. Nurses, doctors could be understandable. They have the overwhelming task to be voyeurs in such sinister places, listening in order to treat those inflicted. However, security guards? What could be so gruesome about carousing drugged zombies? So Norma thinks.

The director slides eyeglasses back up the bridge of his sloped nose. The temple tips flick salt and pepper strands that are covering his ears. He removes a pen from his white hospital coat to sign a medical chart. A line that waves like an ECG (electrocardiogram) appears on the paper. Clicks from the pen sound again and again and again. Norma begins to envision taking the pen from his lanky fingers and snapping it in two, three, perhaps four pieces to make the noise stop. Restraint saves the pen from her growing irritation. "May I?" Norma asks, extending her hand for the noise maker. She takes it and places it on the counter.

Wilbur Wooley, MD, as sewn on the chest of his hospital coat, stands uncomfortably close to Norma. He is much taller, nearly six feet four. Just a half inch shy of being taller than Xavier. Another way they differ is Wilbur is incredibly skinny and a lot less brawny. He watches Norma as she takes a step to gain more social distance between them. He can't see what offends her. Or is it they don't share the same ability to profile. Being an adolescent psychiatric doctor, Norma would hope so… at least to some degree. After all, his degree is much higher than any Norma was ever privy to complete. Yet, he doesn't seem to question why Norma is there, standing head to toe in black with raven hair and ivory skin, looking to be a middle-aged centerfold of *Moms* and *Gothic* magazine.

"This is Elizabeth," he says. Donovan had set this meeting up using an alias Norma is certain to remember. "She's Sarah's aunt. She is here to visit," Dr. Wooley says. He begins to walk off but stops to offer Norma a hand. She shakes it and smirks. A thought suddenly crosses her mind. He kind of resembles Donovan. "It's good for her to have a visitor," Dr. Wooley says.

"Her mother has not been in to see her yet?" Norma asks. She treads carefully. Dr. Wooley has examined Sarah's history very closely. She is confident that Dr. Wooley has heard more than Donovan has seen in a database. Single mother treated numerous times for drug overdose, social worker visits, and trips to the emergency room with suspicious injuries. Norma has been briefed. Where the father is or the exact causes of old scars was not on file. "I'm sorry. I know you can't discuss that," Norma says. It was not necessary to hear the answer spill from Dr. Wooley's mouth when each micro-expression on his face answered Norma. That was her intent all along. It is a hard pill to swallow in this hospital to learn Sarah may be a child first sold into child sex trafficking by the one who made her—sold as if a non-refundable, no-return product.

A nurse leads Norma to room 11. Norma peeks in at a girl, twelve maybe thirteen if she had to guess, sitting with her knees up into her chest on the small cot. She is dressed in a gown as dingy as the room walls, with oil saturating her stringy brown hair—the floor equally grungy. Sarah is staring blankly at the wall as she rocks. Norma releases her empathy in one long sigh. She must not allow Sarah to feel her worry. Norma enters, startling Sarah. "It's okay. It's okay," she reassures. She senses Sarah's anxiety heighten. "It's okay," she repeats calmingly. Norma goes to her bedside and sits at the foot of the bed. "My name is Elizabeth. What's your name?" she asks, attempting to bond. Norma keeps a distance comfortable for Sarah.

"Sarah," she speaks softly. Sarah looks to Norma, then returns her eyes to the wall.

"I wanted to come here to talk with you to see if you can help me… I am part of a very special team that stops the bad men who did this to you. We chase the boogeyman that haunts kids like you. But I don't have much time. Do you think you can help me?" Norma asks.

Sarah ignores Norma and just keeps rocking back and forth, staring at the wall. Her mind appears to Norma to be slipping in and out of her reality. Norma is beginning to believe this will be difficult. Drugs can block even this expert profiler her ability to profile, and Sarah is well beyond one dose of medication. Sarah is on no less a pharmacy assortment to help her cope with the terrors that curse her mind. Donovan has told Norma that at the time of Sarah's rescue, she had proven to be a miracle. Because most kidnapped children, once the narrow window closes, are lost forever. Norma is wondering if the harrowing things Sarah experienced for three years, as to her life now, or even the future hell she will be released into, Sarah would feel it to be a miracle.

Norma sees traces of the pain she endured by the visible scars that cover Sarah's legs and arms. They are nothing compared to invisible scars inside, as Norma once knew all too well.

"I can't say I know how you feel…But I do know how I felt when I was repeatedly raped by different men when I was captured." With little time left to find Charlie, Norma dives quickly. Sarah stops rocking, but her eyes remain on the wall. "Can I tell you a little story?" Norma asks. Sarah does not answer or look at Norma, but Norma can tell Sarah's ears have perked, captivated by her words. "When I was five, I was abandoned by my mom and left with my father, who could be very mean… even cruel. He beat me many, many times and often. When I was about your age, he would force me to strip naked and stand in front him, a mirror, whatever fed his rage. I felt like my soul had been lifted from my body and was stolen from me.

"Did you hate your father?" Sarah asks.

"Yes," Norma says.

"What happened?" Sarah asks, listening intently.

"I learned to survive until the day I could leave him. I was seventeen when I went into the Army to become even tougher, skilled to never let anyone hurt me ever again. I was numb when I needed to be, to cope. It was the only way I knew how to survive. It was like a switch I learned to turn off… I had become so good at it that shortly after joining the Army, I was pulled to become an agent and joined that special team that I told you about earlier, to fight the bad guys and protect kids like you… That switch helped me one day when I was out with my team on a mission and was captured. Right before I had guns pointed in my face, I had ordered my team to safety. I knew I could survive and was prepared for whatever happened to me while I waited for my men to return… Those bad guys repeatedly beat and raped me for hours upon hours…it felt like an eternity. But I didn't give in to them. They were not going to win!" Sarah begins to look at Norma with a tear drop escaping its shackles.

"Are you numb now?" Sarah asks, eager for Norma's response. Norma can see Alex dead on the warehouse floor, then thinks of the lengths she will endure to find Charlie. She thinks of the switch she spoke of. Norma will do well to divert the question.

Norma goes on to share the moment her soul returned to her. The day she met Alex and the day Alexander was born. She tells her more secrets that were once held by pink and purple butterflies—until the day her son found her diary and released her nightmares for all to see.

"Were you mad at him?" Sarah asks.

"No… well maybe…at first. I think I was more embarrassed, ashamed like I did something wrong to deserve it.

Like a penalty for just being born. As if somehow it was all my fault—my mother, my father, those bad men who had captured me."

Sarah scoots close to Norma, then searches deep into Norma's soul. She places a hand on Norma's. She stares harder, then feels to know. "I'm happy you were born. I know you would have protected me if you were my mom," she says. Norma can feel that their bond is complete.

"Sarah, honey, I really need your help." Norma retrieves the picture of Charlie and holds it for her to get a good look at it. "You see this little boy? This is Charlie. We need to protect him from having stories like ours. He is four. Have you ever seen him?"

"No," Sarah says.

"Take a second and look at it closely. Maybe his hair has changed color, his clothes would be different." Sarah takes a second but still gives Norma the same answer. "Can you remember all the places you were taken? Details of the men that held you captive?"

Sarah begins to talk of everything, every man she can remember. She tries hard to recollect the days she was sold to old, middle-aged, younger, elite men and the crowded cages or rooms she was kept in with other young girls and young boys. She painfully revisits being auctioned at desolate buildings, then returned for the gunmen's turn, hair dyed for the buyer's delight, and drugs to keep her from squirming to resist. She was forced to wash away their sins until the smell of torture became unnoticeable. Sometimes even with the sting of cheap perfume on open wounds to mask their foulness. Sarah stops when she recalls the days when sitting was unbearable.

"I'm sorry that happened to you. Sarah… It was not your fault," Norma expresses with conviction. "It was NOT your fault."

Sarah releases her legs and swings around to hug Norma. A little light shines from her eyes. She squeezes tight, then lets go. Norma stands. Information on the tunnel and men was enlightening. Sarah never seeing Charlie is bleak. She thanks her and speaks of bravery. "How did you get your soul back?" Sarah asks.

"I had to reach up and grab it. I was determined when my son was born that no longer would the ones who so wronged me ever take it again… Sarah, those men hurt you terribly physically. I know how that affected me." Norma reaches and grabs Sarah's arm. "But like your arms, legs here. It is just flesh, your physical self. Shell, you can say. It can be hurt and it can heal. The body is amazing. It may leave a scar, but it will mend if you let it. So, too, will your heart, your soul. Let your mind heal. Don't pick it apart. What happened to you, to me… it was not our fault. But it is over. Let it be over. And even if it is to ever happen again, no matter how atrocious, you have your power back to survive. Please, don't let them win." Norma turns to leave.

"Ms. Elizabeth," Sarah calls. With sympathetic eyes, she continues, "I'm sorry for what happened to you, too."

Norma smiles. "Would it be okay if I stop in one day soon to see how you're doing?" Sarah answers excitedly, moving her head up and down. "When I do, we can talk, victorious." Norma can see gaps and cavities in Sarah's teeth as her lips part and cheeks rise.

Sarah stands to walk Norma to the door. Her head is down, saddened by her new friend leaving her so soon. Norma was the drug she needed. "Elizabeth, wait!" she calls out. A memory has come to mind. "I do remember hearing them talk about a blond, blue-eyed boy they captured in Washington, DC. The way they described him was a lot like the boy in the picture you showed me. It was right before we were rescued."

"Are you sure they said Washington, DC?" Norma asks.

"Yes… Blond and blue-eyed boys brought top dollar. If not, they could make even more selling him to people who needed his organs."

"Do you remember what they said happened to him?" Norma persists with caution as disgust sickens to the thought that this young girl was exposed to such atrocities. If not for Charlie, she would not be so persistent for her to remember.

"He was being brought to Mexico. Not far from here. It's the same place I told you about. Where I was held. But I never saw him."

Norma quickly hugs Sarah and rushes to rejoin Atropos. She calls Donovan to instruct him on a task she is certain to make a difference. The clock weighs even heavier on her that time is truly running out. She can hear Charlie's cries. Norma can see the little boy standing, stripped, as his young, innocent soul rises out from his body, pleading to stay. She knows if she doesn't find Charlie soon, he will eventually shoo it away, as he swallows the pain. Norma knows this all too well.

CHAPTER 28

"We've got to find Charlie now. Here," Norma says, tossing her rucksack at David as she climbs into the SUV. Norma shuts the vent that is blowing cool, drying her sweaty skin while she takes the few minutes to catch her breath while they gear up in order to brief Atropos and Donovan on everything Sarah had said and everything Norma could cipher that was left unspoken. "We still can't confirm," Donovan says. Norma goes with her gut and chooses to take a chance on Donovan's earlier words: that it's open and business as usual. For Charlie and these children, she will risk it.

The Atropos men, normally pumped while clips are shoved in, ready for the mission ahead, were now anxious, knowing that over four hours has been lost. They are sweating from more than Southern California's warmer air. Unlike the terrorists they stalk and chase in compounds in remote locations outside of the US, this enemy funding the terrorists in Norma's collection of faces is on the move within their homeland. And they hold priceless shields.

The SUV carrying Norma, Alexander, David, and Xavier stops. The SUV carrying the other Atropos men quickly brakes behind them. They move swiftly, monitoring their surroundings to ensure they are alone and no one is watching. Norma confirms through her headset with Donovan that this is the city drain they will enter. This is the exact spot Craig's team uncovered before. Luckily, the traffickers are unaware it was this entrance on the US side that surveillance watched as they crawled out and rushed the children to a nearby KFC parking lot. If they had known, it would have been clamped off and more time than allotted would be needed to find the new artery of crime. Children were shoved into cars and transported out. It was blocks from this location that Craig's team blocked the road and intercepted, killing the transporter and guard, saving the children—Sarah being one of them. Alexander pulls the handle to slide off the concrete lid. It screeches to reveal a forty-eight-inch solid pipe with small metal steps and no end in sight. He looks to Xavier. "You better suck it in on this one." Xavier shoves Alexander and Raiden to the side to be the first one down this tight rabbit hole. Until now, Raiden, since joining Atropos, has taken point. Xavier tucks the gun into his pants, wraps the utility belt around his neck, and raises the rifle in one hand while the other holds on to the hot metal with each step. He sucks and holds in as much as possible.

"Oh good God," Alexander says, watching as Xavier makes his way down. "We're not going to die from gun bullets. We're all going to die from bullets that shoot from his ass." Norma smiles, then quickly follows Xavier. Claustrophobia will be tested as they step down one by one. Light funnels down where they are crouched waiting for Raiden to take his final step. Before the driver replaces the concrete lid, goggles turn on flashing fluorescent green, yellow, red images into their eyes.

These are the types of tunnels they are familiar with. Many connect under Washington, DC, like the steam pipes that warm the entire city. It comes with no surprise they would be constructed for more than the sake of good—that a need for more than escaping a terrorist threat or safekeeping would exist.

"Craig said look east for the closest tap into this drain. From there we will travel south," Norma says. They begin crawling on their knees, one by one, closely through this damp concrete conduit with rifles now slung to their backs. Their knees and hands soak up water in the drain. Alert rises higher than the ground thirty-nine feet above them. If they come face to face with traffickers, the consequences will be dire. Norma knows by the photos taken during the surveillance that the tunnel tapping into this city drain will allot more room for mobility. They just need to get to it before thermal images that are not Atropos appear. Norma wonders if Alexander, David, Atropos are really beginning to prefer foreign soil. Regardless, she knows they would follow her to the gates of hell. So they continue. Still she wonders how these gates are so close to home.

Xavier abruptly stops, making Norma's head crash into him. "Xavier! If you purposely made my face hit your ass, I will kill you myself," Norma says. Xavier taps her to signal he has found something. It is a circular break in the concrete. A provisional door plugs the hole. Xavier cautiously opens it.

His head gradually peeks in, quietly searching if they would be alone. Finally, he can stretch his legs, although his back will now need to bend. Norma crawls into the boxed tunnel, then stands, slightly ducking to compensate for the three-inch difference. She steps back while Atropos piles in. Norma switches goggles for a Cyclops and a wicked laser light that blinds with over a thousand lumens. The laser scans up from the rail-and-cart system in the dirt floor to up the wood beam that holds parts of the dense clay walls. Each wood beam is T shaped and connected with wires draping from the top. With the lights turned off, it may appear to be abandoned. If not, a flick of a switch will warn them of company. Norma feels air flowing and with it can hear Craig tell her that these tunnels have been equipped with ventilation—even an elevator on the other side. If it is abandoned and the power is out, they may be trapped and forced to return to American soil. Norma speculates about how many Charlies and Sarahs it took to build this. The sophistication demonstrates the determination and monetary resources of these international child traffickers and terrorists.

Atropos begins the three thousand two steps it will take to reach the elevator, with hopes to breach the surface into a concealed industrial area. Lights flicker on, then off—an electrical surge most likely. "Good, those legs of wires are still energized. I can work with that," Vali says. He was brought into Atropos for his outstanding marks as a civil engineer and master electrician… and a hell of a sniper eye.

"Do you have a plan?" David asks Norma.

"Yes. Find Charlie and kill these motherfuckers for what they have done… If I had known before that this is what funded the terrorist cell that killed Alex, I would have cut Chris Logan's dick off while he was alive and fed it to him."

"Alrighty, then," David says. "You have a plan." David looks over to Alexander and two sets of pearlescent whites shine through the dark.

"Eighty-six terrorist jihads on the wall, eighty-six terrorist jihads..."

"Shut up, Xavier," rings through the channel from all but Norma. As said many times before, since the beginning, Norma has accepted Xavier's wit and has secretly favored his weapon to combat the evils that face them. She thinks of Dorian and the constant bickering he and Xavier would have over counting bodies and who would win their contest. All the lost souls of Atropos crowd her mind with one that stands in the forefront. She misses Alex oh so much.

Alexander looks to his watch to see the steps taken. They are halfway there, and so far it has been a straight shot south. So the watch says. Silence gives way to boots stomping rails, rifles occasionally shuffling from one hand to the other, and nylon utility belts swaying with their stuffed cartridges and knives on their hips. Their breath echoes as they pant the warm, damp, musty air. Alexander looks and reads: 2,185. They are closer. Less than a quarter-mile to go. Brows are wiped by clinging gloves.

"Norma. What if he's not there?" David asks.

"What if we can't find him?" Alexander asks.

"We will find that boy if I have to peel every layer of this earth to interrogate the devil himself."

2,871 Alexander's watch reads. Norma moves to the front of Xavier. She slows feeling to be close. Her feet stop and she turns to face her men. "Vali," she calls forward. Vali rushes between the two lines to join Norma by her side. Pulleys can be heard, then a light bulb flickers on. Norma looks to Vali. "Fall back," she says. Xavier starts to retake his lead until Norma points him back to Alexander and David. Weapons ready and aim. Sniffles echo, then a harsh voice warns for silence. She listens to the voices. Her finger rises to signal one. How many children she cannot assess, as footsteps draw near. Atropos pushes their backs tight against the walls, ready to give the children a passageway to run past them. The gunman sees Norma and takes off back to the elevator. Norma begins to chase to stop him before he makes it up that shaft, alerting others. She jumps on his legs, knocking him and her to the ground. He spins, trying to fire a round into her chest. They struggle for the gun. Norma flips sideways as his gun discharges, firing a round into the tunnel's ceiling. She grabs the barrel with one hand and uses the other to break his wrist. She pulls her head back, then uses it to break the bridge of his nose. He grabs her by the throat and begins to squeeze hard, choking her. Norma begins to gurgle. Brut for brut, Norma was no match. Skilled agility and swiftness, he was no match. She can see Alexander, David, and Xavier rushing to her rescue. Norma waves them away. Her arms crisscross his arm that is tightly gripping her neck and jerks as she flips to his side. His arm snaps. Norma reaches for old trusty on her back. The knife goes to his neck. "Where are the other children?" she demands. Nothing. He bends his head back, giving her a clear cut. "Oh no, you disgusting bastard. You are not getting off that easy. Where did you get these children from?" She questions him rolling Spanish out with a fluent tongue.

His tense eyes stare to the ceiling, then look deep into hers as she straddles, pinning him down. "Vali," she calls. "Can you splice one of those wires and connect it to him and your portable power outlet?"

"Oh, this is going to be fun," Xavier says.

David kneels before the oldest of the trembling children. She looks to be eleven. "Have you seen this boy?" he asks, showing her a picture of Charlie. "Please look closely." She nods yes.

"When?" he asks.

Her face is stunned and appears to have cried her last tear. She mumbles, "Four days ago." David's expression is confused. "Is he here with you now?"

She shakes her head no.

"Do you know where they took him?" Again, she shakes her head no.

"Okay, I want you to take this flashlight and all of you get out of here. Follow this tunnel until you can't anymore. You will see a circular hole and a door. Open it, go right, and crawl until you see stairs. Go up, then wait. A man named Craig will open the drain lid and help you out… Can you do it?" he asks. The girl nods and releases her tears. She begins to sob. David wipes her face. "You are safe now. You're going home… Now go!" He watches with Craig on the phone pressed to his ear until the last little body is no longer within eyesight. David comes around to Norma.

The man squirms, forcing old trusty to slice the first layer of his neck. His fight is futile. His gun has been stripped, as has any chance he will escape her. Soon he will be tied to flickering voltage.

“Hook him up,” Norma says. Xavier yanks him off the floor and takes his turn to pin him to the wall. Milo breaks pieces of wood and jars his mouth open. Vali pulls his tongue out from his mouth, then clamps one wire to it and one to the portable electrical outlet. This may not kill him, but it will definitely make him wish he was dead. Norma grabs a water bottle from her rucksack. She takes a swig, then pours a small amount into her hand to rinse the sweat from her face. She pours the remainder over his tongue, then feet. “Turn it on,” she says. Xavier lets go just as the man’s body begins to shake with current coursing through him. “Enough,” she says. Vali turns it off and the man falls to the ground, shaking. “Does that help energize your tongue to find words? Do you want to tell me now?”… Nothing. “Again,” she says. “More!” Vali makes adjustments, then cranks the power back on. The man shakes harder as his eyes begin to bulge. He screams. He was not trained to withstand anyone over five feet tall. He was a transporter.

“I’ll tell you. I’ll tell you!” his trembling voice yells. After all was said about fake passports for the children exported, forged birth certificates, dyed hair, forced organ harvesting from live children, then finally confirmation that Charlie had been there but does not know where Charlie is now, Norma turns her back on him to walk to the elevator. “Kosmo and Lander, search his pockets, then take him to Craig,” Norma says. “We’ll wait for you here.” Lander removes a cell phone from the gunman’s pocket and tosses it to Norma.

“What the fuck? Are you serious?” Xavier yells. “You’re going to let this asshole live? When did we start taking piece of shit prisoners?”

"He's a transporter. Craig can use him to get more intel. Let them figure out what to do with him. We don't have time for this," Norma commands.

David and Alexander walk to Norma's side, leaving Xavier to huff dissatisfaction to a painless ending. Xavier pushes Kosmo and Lander to the side before they remove the wire. He reaches and grabs the control from Vali's hand, cranking it on and up. The gunman drops, convulsing, as currents flow through. Xavier turns it off, looking to Norma. "Oops," he says. Xavier steps on the gunman's chest as he strides toward Norma.

"Did you hear what he and that the little girl said?" David asks.

"I caught it," Alexander says. He begs for Norma to look. "They said four days ago. The picture of him in that bunker puts him there two days ago." Alexander glances to David to confirm that he agrees. Alexander counts the days backwards. "He was brought here first. He was moved from here to the bunker at the hotel we just left." Norma turns and resumes walking to the elevator. "Where are you going?" Alexander says. They are moving backward. They need to catch up. Charlie has been missing six days now.

"There are children up there, and we know *where* they are." Norma stands at the elevator waiting for Kosmo and Lander to return. "We can't leave them!"

The elevator doors open and Norma steps out into the small industrial building with gun drawn. Like stuffed sardines, the five men burst out, then point rifles down, scanning the room. They wait for the elevator to return with the others.

A Spaniard man enters the room with his hands up. "I am a keeper!" he shouts. His English rolls with a heavy accent. "My name is Gael. Donovan sent me. Thanatos." His password is approved. The rifles are lowered. Norma had changed it just hours before they left. Keeping all things Greek mythology, she chose Thanatos—the son of Nyx and the personification of death.

"Where exactly are we?" Norma asks.

"You are next to the Tijuana National Airport. Donovan has scheduled me here to help you. You will need someone that blends with locals to guide you in." He looks at the mavericks dressed in arsenal, certain to stand out. "You will need to leave your rifles and equipment here." He walks over and waves for his help through what looks to be a hole in the crumbling wall. The sound of a handle clicking open can be heard, then the keeper's helper steps out. "Leave them with Antonio," he says.

One by one they stack their rifles on top of each other. Then headpieces, goggles, and rucksacks are tossed in. "Is this safe?" Norma asks. Gael reassures Norma that since the last bust near the US entrance into the tunnel, no one knows that this place has been discovered by the US agencies except for US agents. But once they leave these doors, the keeper has or knows nothing. No matter, Atropos will not need his services outside of these walls. Norma has extracted the information she needs from the transporter and each of them is fluent in several languages—Spanish of course being one of them.

"We need to find a market nearby," Norma says. The man we caught in the tunnel said they are being held near here at a market. We are not going to be able to stay together. David,

Alexander with me. Xavier, you and Lander keep a safe distance. Milo, Vali, and Raiden, you'll flock through the market. You are frat boys on vacation. Stefen, Kosmo, and Nick, you scatter but keep close. Norma looks at the keepers. "Do you have pesos?" Gael pulls his wallet out from his pants and hands pesos to her. Norma grabs it, then disburses it to the men. "You stay here… Let's go, men."

Norma, Alexander, and David walk minutes ahead of Xavier and Lander through the alleyway. They step onto the sidewalk of a main street. Norma grabs David's hand as Alexander leads ahead. Norma follows the directions given to her by the man in the tunnel. Two blocks then a left and the market will be in sight. Norma begins to crave the shock combat she so prefers. Rush in, sweep, eliminate the threat, then retreat. This will require more finesse, more patience.

It is not but a minute before reaching the market that Alexander is approached. A Mexican man tries to seduce him into a tented area in what Alexander feels is like a circus carnie hustling for more customers. Norma and David follow close by as Alexander pretends to be interested. The Mexican man is offering him his greatest pleasures. He could choose. Older? Younger? Girl? Boy? Alexander fakes caution as if the Mexican man is posing undercover, leading him to a sting arrest. He repeats asking what is his pleasure. He tells Alexander that a boy could be his for just two thousand pesos. Alexander swallows his repulsion and smiles as he ponders his true greatest pleasure. To have *this* man's ass impaled. Alexander continues to sell his nervous caution. The Mexican man is buying.

Alexander pulls a tarp back and is taken aback. There are rows of makeshift portable rooms with small cots filled with children of all types, all ages, boys and girls. He walks past a room with a Hispanic boy pressing his hand against the wire mesh window. Alexander visualizes his son, as he and Norma are convinced it will be, and he sickens with rage. He stops and places his hand against the boy's, touching through the mesh. "I'll take him," Alexander says. The Mexican man turns away and begins to shout.

"You need to leave!"

Alexander turns to see Norma and David approaching. Norma gives him a name from the intel intercepted and tells him they were sent here to adopt a blond-headed son. She holds David's hand as tears force out, telling the convincing story of being sterile and the auction they failed to win. He interrupts her performance as his cell phone rings. Norma can see his anger as his words translate fluently to her. She watches as his fury rages higher. He has been warned of the bunker raid at the hotel and the four dead guards found. Norma profiles the suspicion that's rising in this man. He looks back to Alexander, who's fanning two thousand pesos in his hand, luring him to come back.

Norma begins to weep louder, burying her face into David's chest. "Let's just leave. I'll tell Abdul he was wrong. The boy he promised isn't here." Norma is sure the dead doppelganger isn't calling to alert anyone, seeing for herself, Abdul's body chilling on ice at the agency.

"Wait here," he yells, walking back for Alexander to give him the pesos.

Alexander waits for him to turn and walk back to Norma and David. He makes eye contact with Norma. All appear unsure as to how this will end. Alexander steps in the room and begins to quickly speak to the boy. "I'm not going to hurt you." The boy is scared and begins to cry wildly. Alexander speaks to him in Spanish.

"You have cocaine?" the boy asks in English. He fidgets off the bed. "Please. They usually give me cocaine. I'm scared."

"Listen. Calm down. I'm not going to hurt you. I'm here to get you out. But we need to hurry." English or Spanish, the boy does not listen—he only hears the screams he feels to be next. Alexander watches the boy pace back and forth, begging for cocaine, anything to ease the pain he is sure to endure. The boy will need to be forced out, Alexander feels certain.

Norma rushes in. "Let's get them out of here now!" In the time Alexander had been in there, Norma had chosen her preferred method after all. Alexander and the boy step over dead bodies as Atropos collects children from each makeshift room. She opens the door to the last one, but it was too late. The young girl, perhaps ten, is dead with blood coming from every hole. "God damn it," Norma yells, hitting the wall. "Get her! We're not leaving her. We're taking her home!"

With handguns flashing, pointing, Atropos speeds the children until they reach the small industrial building. Norma spots the keepers, Gael and Antonio. They are all safe but one. Norma hopes that in all the haste it left locals in the market square unable to recall a single detail or offer any description. Anyone who could lays dead on the market square floor.

CHAPTER 29

Norma tosses everything into the SUV and slams the door. They have made it back to the California side. She pounds the dashboard, angry. "Fuck, fuck, fuck!" she repeatedly yells. Craig is with Atropos outside of the drain manhole, quickly shuffling children into a van. Only this time they are headed to a hospital where they will be reunited with crying parents while one enters the morgue. Norma can't remove the image of the little girl lying on the cot with eyes fixed open. She thinks of Charlie, then her grandbaby, and feels darkness creep in. She is certain that old trusty would be dripping wet from anyone in her path if that had been her bloodline on that cot. She is certain that old trusty will be from here on out. Charlie's picture is removed from her pocket. She sits staring at his sparkled eyes and cheesy smile. Her head begins to throb, hurting as she hears Alexander's words that they may never find him. They have been moving backward and are left with no lead to resume. The bunker—Charlie was seen there two days ago. The market, four days ago. *Where are you?* She speaks to Charlie. Norma pulls out the gunman's cell phone and attempts to crack his password. It flashes to try again. A variable hits her, remembering the Mexican man in the market conversation. "Shit," she says, feeling it has been missed.

Norma jumps out from the SUV, opens the trunk, and lowers the tailgate. She calls Atropos and Craig to join her. While she waits for the last child to be loaded and driven away, Norma calls Donovan for help. "Hold one," she instructs Donovan on the phone. Alexander is first to join her. "Get your laptop," she says.

Alexander reaches into his bag and pulls the laptop out. He places it on the tailgate. The screen turns on, prompting for his credentials. "What are we looking for?" he asks.

"How to find Charlie," she says. David joins Norma's side, then the remaining Atropos circle around her. Norma calls Craig to come quickly. "Where is the gunman from the tunnel?" she asks as he runs to her.

"We are holding him near a US consulate office on the other side. He's in Tijuana," Craig says.

Norma begins to playback Charlie's journey aloud. "Connect this cell phone to your laptop." Norma commands Alexander to move with lightning speed. "When we were in the market the man with us received a phone call alerting him of the bunker raid. I don't believe the gunman in the tunnel told us everything. He knows more than he said…If the man in the market was alerted, that means they all are in contact. I need to get into his phone for the numbers he's called and received." Alexander leaves the cursor to Donovan as he navigates on his laptop to trick the gunman's cell phone. Donovan breaks in and the calls are downloaded. The numbers dialed and received are nameless. Donovan searches the database but finds nothing. Not one name is connected to these numbers. Donovan tells Norma the numbers are from prepaid phones and are impossible to trace.

"I need to spend a little time with the transporter," Norma tells Craig.

"Do you have your passports?" Craig asks. Donovan and Norma predicted a time that a quick jump on the helicopter would not be sensible—nor the pilot touching the stealth helicopter down amidst locals. How viral videos from cell phones couldn't be taken down before alerting others.

"Yes. Take me to him now," Norma demands. Xavier likes the idea of another chance to crank up voltage.

One then the other, they head for the border. The trailing SUV's engine screams to keep up.

CHAPTER 30

"Where is this boy?" Norma yells, shoving Charlie's picture into the gunman's face. "Where's Charlie?" The gunman smirks, convinced that Norma will not be allowed to pick up where she left off in that tunnel. He sits in this room safely inside his country with eyes all around. The blood from his broken nose has dried and is flaking; his tongue, wrist, and arm are swollen and covered with shades of reds and blues. He holds his engorged wrist close to his chest with back pushed against the seat. A cocky smirk has not left his face. "Where is the boy?" she repeats, angry. His persistence riles her. Norma grabs his broken wrist then pulls him forward. She slams it on the table. He grunts. She forces it down while the gunman struggles. His inflexibility is going to be tested. Norma gestures for Xavier to come close. She nods down to the gunman's wrist. Xavier smiles, then chops brutally down onto the gunman's broken wrist as Norma lets go. The gunman screams as confidence begins to shatter. Norma places his cell phone in front of him. "What number do you call for a pick-up for the children trafficked through that tunnel?" He retracts his crushed bones into his chest and rocks in pain. His eyes water from the agony he feels. "What number oversees the house and bunker under the hotel?" Norma would bet the owner of that house that Craig captured may be dead, but the one in charge is not. All intel has shown that dangerous leaders hide in safe houses.

The gunman closes his quivering lips, sealing his swollen tongue in tight. Norma takes old trusty from its sheath and rips the gunman's shirt. She hits him in the diaphragm, forcing the wind out, then stuffs his shirt into his open mouth to muffle what he can only fear will happen next. Norma pulls his broken arm out and forces it onto the table. She nods for Xavier again. This time Alexander pushes Xavier to the side for his chance to give the gunman a taste of the pain the boy must have endured...but for the gunman, cocaine will not be offered.

Craig leaves the room, giving Atropos their privacy, knowing this team's capacity surpasses his own.

Alexander takes old trusty from Norma's hand. "Where is the boy? Where is Charlie?" he asks calmly. The room goes silent. Alexander raises the knife high, giving it the force it needed to pierce straight through his arm and into the wood table. The gunman screams through the muffling shirt, then gags with certainty the soil beneath them will not save him. His arm remains knifed to the table staining the oak wood red. Still nothing. Again, Alexander jerks the knife free from the table and bone, then raises it higher to drive it through his arm and into the table. The gunman yowls. Norma was right.

He was not trained to withstand anyone over five feet tall. He was a transporter.

He talks, giving the names for each number, the destinations near international ports that children are smuggled through. Finally, he tells the rumor of a mansion in upstate New York where he heard the blond boy was destined to be trafficked. He leaves nothing on the table but his bleeding arm, spilling all to Norma that he overheard the boy was there for a passport to Russia. Charlie was to be shipped off to a wealthy family in need of a boy's heart. Harvesting fresh would ensure a successful transplant and, in this foul thieving manner, the wait times are extremely short. No documentation is ever found for black market organ theft as they board in New York, on private planes, crossing the Atlantic into Europe for faster delivery. Norma prays that Charlie's heart isn't at rest in a small red cooler, chilling while waiting for the final flight before it can beat again.

Norma leans down to whisper in the gunman's ear. David, Alexander, and Xavier read her lips as Norma forms the words *I'll be back for you.* Norma straightens her back, then her jacket. "Get the chopper here," she calls out. "We need to get to New York." Passports will not be needed. Donovan has cleared them for takeoff. "You have from West to East to find that damn mansion," she tells Donovan before hitting the end call button.

CHAPTER 31

The time tells Norma that it is depleted. It has been six days, nine hours, and eleven minutes since Charlie was taken. Atropos has been scuttling through dirt bunkers and earthen tunnels, eliminating thieving rats, yet only saving fifty-two children. Norma can feel hope for Charlie's recovery slipping away as she's aware the seventy-two hour window has long been closed. She can hear Craig's briefing and count how many times forty seconds has passed since Charlie has been missing. *Every forty seconds a child is kidnapped. That is thirteen thousand seven hundred eighty-six more children kidnapped since Charlie was taken,* she figures against the fifty-two returned. She can feel their fear run through her as fear for Charlie heightens.

Norma's pensive eyes stare out the helicopter window. She looks down as they pass over houses with lights beginning to turn on and streets with bustling cars eager to return home for a family dinner, wondering if a stolen child is caged deep beneath them or are they in a grave disposition without a loved one anywhere in sight. The blades chuff into the sunset, crossing state after state, as Atropos sits, dismal. Norma thinks of the hours it has taken them to arrive in New York and figures how many more children that figures to be.

"Stop it," David says. He can see and feel the blame she's loaded down with on the helicopter. "This is not your fault."

"I will find that boy," Norma says, determined that blame does not end with this ride. "He will return to his mother—no matter how." Norma is certain she will cross international waters if needed. She destroyed the terrorist cell; now she will destroy and capture their markets of funding. This mission has been like none before it. Targeted faces shifting and improvising is typical for Norma and the Atropos team. They were elite as proved by every successful mission. Norma flipping the switch on and off only to hold it in the middle as she searches for Charlie is not. Norma lives in black or white. She is feeling Alexander to be right. She and old trusty may soon retire. How she wishes for Alex by her side. *Focus,* she thinks. *Where are you, Charlie*?

CHAPTER 32

The helicopter hovers in the dusky air to the far rear of the mansion in Saratoga Springs, New York. The trees sway from side to side, dusting the ground below with a light blanket of snow. The pilot touches down safely near the tree line into the woods. Norma instructs the pilot to leave quickly and find a spot at the nearby Albany International Airport to wait for her signal. It is less than twenty-three miles away and will only take minutes when called to return. Donovan has called ahead and clears him for landing.

Atropos jumps from the helicopter and runs into the tree line for cover. They wait to see who emerges from this stately mansion just to be certain that Donovan was successful with tripping security codes, giving them time to penetrate the house unnoticed. "Are you with us?" she whispers into the headset to Donovan.

"Roger," he confirms.

"Can you see inside?" The house is too far for the naked eye to see in. The optic eye only sees shadows through sheer drapes and dim lighting.

"That's a negative," he says. His attempt to crack into the mansion's inside cameras has been unsuccessful. Donovan comes in clear; once through the mansion window, they will be on their own.

"What is this place?" Alexander asks. He zooms in closer to spy inside the windows, but it's in vain. He scopes the outside. "It looks like a resort." The massive gray stone reaching three stories high with wood trim and tower-topped looks to be a Queen's estate. The security fences and gates ensure anyone not invited does not disturb its guests. Norma, David, and the remaining team zoom in as much of the fifty-four thousand square foot structure the Cyclops eye would allow them to see. They rake over the elaborate gardens as they wait to confirm they are alone.

"How has no one been suspicious of child traffickers and terrorists?"

Donovan quickly answers Alexander. An international Russian banker holds the deed, a socialite who throws money to the townspeople and parades the streets in a Lamborghini for all to assume his impervious power. He contributes generously to local children's causes to veil the evils that hide behind awarded bronze plaques that hang nicely on the walls of this mansion. Fundraisers have been hosted here with children running freely while stolen children are held captive somewhere below happy feet. When charity is not the mask he's wearing, you must be a buyer or a collector to enter through his doors. Atropos stands sure there have been a few marked terrorists hiding behind those walls, with Chris Logan coming to mind.

"This is going to be difficult," David says, seeing the snowy ground that they will need to cover. Tracks are sure to be seen if drapes open for a peek outside. David picks up two evergreen branches that have fallen and hands one to Lander and one to Nick. They are to sweep the snow as they trail behind. "Let's go," he says. Norma orders them to remain a second longer. A vision of the earthen tunnels and wire cages comes to her mind. Her gut tells her that there will be no pitter-patter of young feet warmed from imported marble floors. There will be no trains, planes, or ballerinas plastered on children's bedroom walls. For the children they seek, Norma sees a dark dungeon with cold musky air. She can picture fearing eyes blackened by the desolate horror around them. Her thought limits the footage to whatever is underground.

"If Charlie or any child is here, they are in cellars," Norma says. "In one." She sets them in motion across the vast yard taking cover when available, pointing rifles toward the mansion as Lander and Nick sweep behind them. They creep forward toward the back of the mansion with rifles ready, then stop at a window just aboveground. Norma can hear an alarm blaring from the front gate. "Donovan," she whispers.

"Roger that," Donovan confirms.

Shrubs hide their positions as Kosmo makes his way to the window, crouching for cover. He is her lead weapons man and an explosive expert. This will be their first test of Donovan's success to deactivate the alarms on the windows. Kosmo takes a glass blade and removes enough to pry open the window. They stall, waiting for a sound to alert anyone inside that death has come for them. So they hope the reaper does not get this wrong. They are Atropos. They decide fate. However, Norma knows all too well—that isn't always the story.

One by one, rifle then Atropos, crawl in, with Raiden bringing up the rear. Xavier reaches his hand to help him down as the other hand holds the window open. Xavier touches the eight-foot ceiling to gauge its thickness. Footsteps can be heard telling them what might be trouble above. Goggles flip down, then switch to thermal vision. If there are warm bodies, they will see them through the dark spaces.

Atropos flanks with Norma, demanding the lead as rifles point forward. Handles slowly turn to open only to reveal childless rooms. With each opened door all that can be found are overly stuffed storage rooms. Atropos turns a corner of the basement, seeing a light peeking from underneath the door. The air turns humid. The door knob turns slowly. Light bursts out from the cracked door. Norma peeks in and sees a wooden bench with towels rolled and stacked in a pyramid, then two large glass doors sweating from within. She barely spots through the clouds of moist air a salt-and-pepper haired man sitting with his head leaning back against the wall with only a white towel wrapped around his bulging waist; otherwise he would be nude. Norma shuts the door, leaving Stefen to attend the sweltering man if he were to leave. Xavier raises his hands, questioning as to why he can't eliminate him now before becoming a threat. Norma shakes her head, denying him the pleasure, then signals them to follow. There are more rooms to search, and time is feared to have ended to find Charlie.

They open the adjacent door, and a cold breeze wafts over them. It is an immense wine cellar with racks and racks of wine, liquor, and a tall glass refrigerator standing in a corner. They can see inside the glass panels a red travel cooler. Norma has a sickening feeling overwhelm her. She gestures for Nick to open the refrigerator door, then Milo to take the cooler out. Milo rolls back the lid to see a small heart and what appears to be a liver packed on dry ice. They feel to know what, or who, it is. Usually strong stomachs turn weak. Xavier rushes back out the door with Alexander and David on foot, knowing where Xavier was headed. David reaches for Xavier's arm to pull him back, but Xavier shrugs him free. Xavier is steaming more robust than the room he is approaching.

Stefen is shoved to the side as Xavier busts through the door. The man startles inside the steam room. He stands and the towel drops. The man reaches for the glass door, yelling as Xavier swings it open. Xavier steps in and with his knife quickly silences the man with one slice across the neck. Blood swirls with water, then runs down around Xavier's feet and down the drain.

Footsteps can be heard stomping the stairs.

David looks to Alexander and Stefen to get Xavier back to the team. Soon they will have company. Norma meets them in the hallway. She motions for them to grab the body as she uses the man's towel to cover the spilled blood on the steam room floor. More towels are loosely dropped in, covering Xavier's rage. Atropos takes the dead man into the wine cellar to hide behind racks of cooling wine bottles. They drop the body to chill while they prepare for whoever discovers them. Voices can be heard calling what they suspect was the man's name. Norma goes to the farthest wall adjoining an unsearched room where words can be heard riling in anger. She absorbs the sounds of high-pitched sniffles. Her hand hits the wall. Children are in there. Norma's eyes flare at Xavier. Her rifle rises with the anxiety of another missed opportunity.

Norma leads Atropos through the door and into the hallway. They dodge bullets as the gunmen shoot. Norma watches as the gunmen snatch and hustle children from the room to push up the stairs while they yell for help. Their rifles stand down, unable to make a clear shot. Atropos follows quickly in pursuit, hearing crying children being pushed and shoved above them. Xavier is first up the steps, with Norma, David, and Alexander following closely. The remaining team quickly joins them on the top of the steps.

Norma commands: "Lander, Kosmo, and Stefen… search every room on the east side. Vali, Milo, and Nick…search the west." The team separates as Norma, Alexander, David, Xavier, and Raiden follow the gunmen through the massive foyer, then toward double doors to the back of the mansion. As the door swings wide for the last gunman to enter the kitchen, Norma can see them huddled around children.

Bullets sound throughout the house, ricocheting off walls as Norma waits to hear confirmation through her headset that the east and west are all clear. Alexander and David move to where they think the gunmen's only other exit remains unguarded. Children can be heard frantically weeping as the gunmen shout for them to shut up. Her attack is measured and weighed against variable scenarios of killed gunmen with children hurt or, worse, killed by their blazing rifles. This time shock combat cannot be risked.

"All clear," Milo confirms into her ear. A few more loud rounds are fired off, then: "All clear," sounds again. Her voice follows theirs through the headset that a liftoff will be needed.

"Roger that," Donovan says.

Xavier is edging to rush the kitchen. Any child in this house is in there. Norma can hear Sarah's tormenting words of Charlie's poached heart for the black market—destined to a wealthy Russian family. "Go get that cooler," she tells Raiden as the men begin to rejoin her. Norma waits for the faceoff with the gunmen hunkering inside the kitchen. Soon Raiden returns with the red and white cooler. They can hear dangerous voices on the other side of the door yelling to join them now. Norma positions Atropos. A door can be heard opening from inside the kitchen as more men join the four gunmen. It has to be an exit to the back of the mansion, remembering the door when they crept to cellar window. David raises his fingers to count off seven.

Distant scuffling can be heard, then silence in the kitchen sets Atropos in motion. "Xavier," Norma calls. Her angry smirk excites Xavier as she nods permission for Xavier to ignite the wicks in Vali's bag.

"Xavier. Knock my socks off!"

Xavier and Vali rush to the foyer as Norma and the team slowly enter the kitchen. David and Alexander rush to the back window while the others sweep the kitchen. "Norma look," David calls. Norma looks out the window at their helicopter hovering. The gunmen and children are running toward it.

CHAPTER 33

"GO, GO, GO!" Xavier commands Atropos out of the mansion.

"*BOOM*," blows Atropos forward as the mansion of ghastly iniquity explodes, then crumbles down. The massive explosion sends huge blazing fireballs and plumes of smoke into the cold gray sky.

They move swiftly across the vast backyard with rifles drawn, chasing the gunmen that are ushering the children to the idling helicopter. The pilot assigned to Atropos is face down in the snow. He is dead. One of the gunmen has taken his seat. Another gunman has taken the seat beside him, waiting for fellow gunmen and hustling children to catch up and be loaded.

Norma stops. She raises her rifle and eyes through the scope, putting a running gunman in her crosshairs. As he runs with a child gripped tightly under his arm, the child comes in and out of her sights. Unable to gain the clear shot, she lowers it, avoiding the chance for the child to be killed in the line of fire. “Steady men!” They slow to wait her command as they alternate the rifles up and down from their eyes. They are still too far away and the amber light emitting from the fire is beginning to vanish as they move farther into the dark. “Move!” Norma sprints off, seeing the children get smaller. As her legs burn faster, the adrenaline fuels them to move even quicker. She can see some are taller, some very young, some white, some black, some brown, all innocent and afraid. From a distance Norma catches a glimpse of a young, fair-skinned boy with blond hair.

Xavier sees what Norma sees and takes the lead, eager for a chance to get close enough to fire off the intended rounds for the gunmen and to use his body for cover. If the terrorists make it to the helicopter, those children will be lost forever. A little girl’s arm is gripped tight as she is being dragged. She stumbles, falling. The gunman yanks her to her feet and scolds her to keep up. Another child trips, breaking his hold, and falls even harder into the snow. One of the gunmen quickly goes to her, then snatches her hair to pull her up. Norma knows what that must feel like. The gunmen turn and fire their guns toward Atropos, missing. Norma, Alexander, Xavier, and the rest of the Atropos men ignite their legs for speed. As less of the field spans between them, another child drops hard to the ground, only this time he is shot to silence. Norma can see clearly this dark-haired boy was not Charlie. Still, the tragedy leaves her heart pained—as to the Atropos men.

The last child is shoved into the helicopter, then the gunmen begin to board. Norma stops. She positions her body, then raises her rifle to aim. A deep breath is drawn in, then held. A single round sounds off, hitting the head of the gunman sitting in the pilot's seat. A second one rapidly leaves the chamber, instantly killing the co-pilot. Their bodies slump forward. Her feet take flight until she catches Atropos.

The gunmen jump out of the helicopter, returning fire. Raiden drops to the ground, losing control of the cooler. He has been hit just above his Kevlar vest with a bullet severing his jugular vein. A fountain of red spurts from his neck. Milo, like Xavier, a decorated combat medic, runs to Raiden, but it is hopeless. After a few gurgles, Raiden is dead. Milo grabs the cooler and takes cover. He knows Norma will not leave this young heart behind. Charlie, or whoever it may be, will return to the mother who gave him, or her, life; no matter what, no matter how.

Atropos nears the helicopter, then stops in a standoff as children are taken out to become human shields. Norma's eyes lock onto the little blond boy who is squirming to break free. "Charlie," she yells. The gunman shouts, blocking her voice from his ear. "Charlie," Norma yells louder as the boy fights the man's hold. He struggles to break free, and Norma's calls go unanswered. "Your mommy Elizabeth sent me! Charlie!" she screams. The boy stops squirming and looks up. It is him! They've found him. Her eyes beg to him to find courage. "Run," Norma screams louder, opening her arms to him. He wiggles, then twists free and runs toward her. A gunman's rifle rises, aiming for a shot at Charlie's back. Alexander throws a knife, sticking it precisely between the gunman's eyes that are aimed with malice. Alexander, the natural-born leader, shows ready to fill her shoes. He's as good as she's trained him to be.

Charlie runs quickly to Norma and jumps straight into her arms. She hugs and kisses his head, then begins to slide him down, attempting to place him behind her. His grip is too tight. He refuses to let go of her. “I know you’re scared. Your mom sent us to get you,” she whispers. She peels him off and forces his grip free. “You have to trust me. I need you to get behind me.” Charlie hides behind Norma’s legs. Now they must get the remaining children to safety. A battle of wills ensues. The gunmen begin to fire rapidly. Atropos scatters, dodging as bullets lodge deep into Kevlar. Norma scoops up Charlie, shifting him to her left side to shield him as she runs to take cover near a tree. The rest fire back, shooting high. Only one gunman drops dead to the ground.

“We’ve got to get those kids away from them,” David yells.

Norma again places Charlie behind her. He clutches her legs tight. She knows that if she tries to run again, she may not be able to protect him. Charlie may be exposed long enough to be caught in the roaring crossfire. She was lucky that he wasn’t hit the last time. Norma assesses each of the kids as they look back, frightened, stiff, and crying numbly. She calls out to the gunmen to give up the kids, and they will leave them unharmed. “We know you are almost out of ammunition,” she warns. “You have nowhere to go.” They watch as one of the gunmen boards the helicopter, pulls the dead pilot from his seat, then prepares for the vertical takeoff. The helicopter hovers slightly above the ground.

Xavier knows Norma’s ploy. He will get his chance for vengeance if they can find a way to get the children to safety. Rifles wave on standby for Norma’s order. The kids’ hair blows, and sniffles are drowned out by spinning rotors. Charlie is safe, but time is running out for the rest of these children. Their eyes cry for Norma's help. She can see their bleak souls leaving, taken away into the dark sky. As the gunmen wave their rifles, studying their options, so, too, does Norma. She can feel each desperate plea penetrate her deeply as the helicopter whisks cold air. She'd better act now. A game she played with Alexander as a small child comes to mind. It may work, she feels. It will work, her gut tells her.

"All right, boys and girls," Norma yells, commanding loudly over the whirling *chuff-chuff-chuff-chuff.* "Simon says be a noodle and drop to the ground."

Together the kids go limp and drop to the ground. Bullets zing over their heads, then bodies of dead gunmen fall all around them. The helicopter begins to take off. Xavier races to jump in. Norma can see Xavier through the windshield, ignoring his own advice and toying with his prey, taunting him that he has a chance to escape. When bored, tired of his own game, Xavier takes his knife and ends the flight. He jumps out onto the snow covered in victory. Little eyes stare, horrified, while Atropos looks on with smiling eyes.

"What?" Xavier yells. "Ooooh, Simon said drop like a limp noodle! I thought you said dead noodle. My bad!"

Atropos rallies the children as Charlie clings to Norma. He feels comfort in her warm arms. David and Alexander walk to Norma, relieved Charlie is safe, the children have been recovered, and finally they all can go home. It's over.

"Well done, Mom," Alexander says.

"Make sure that heart goes home with us," she says with her heart beginning to slow.

Alexander can see she's drained, and exhaustion is all over her pale face. "No more missions for you," he says. He has been right from the beginning; she needs to leave these death-defying missions to the men of Atropos. "You're going to be a grandma now."

Pride from that thought is obvious by her loving smile. Norma squeezes Charlie tightly for a comforting hug, then gently kisses his forehead. "You're okay now. Your mommy is going to be so very happy to see you." She looks to Alexander with tired eyes, ready to go home, understanding that this is, in fact, her last mission.

"Let me have him," Alexander says, reaching to take Charlie from Norma's arms. He refuses to let go. Charlie squeezes her even tighter, his trust forever altered.

"Let me see if he'll come to me," David offers, extending his arms out to Charlie.

Charlie shakes his head no, then buries his face deep into Norma's shoulder, hiding as he shivers. Norma speaks to him calmly, remembering how she used to soothe Alexander when he was four years old. He squirms on her hip for a better hold, forcing her to nearly lose balance. Norma grunts. "I need you to go with him now. I don't think I will be able to carry you much longer." Norma points to Alexander. "You see that man right there? He is one of the good ones. I know that because he is my son." Charlie peeks at Alexander. "Go to him now."

Charlie turns to Alexander with his arms wide open. Alexander reaches and takes him from Norma. Blood has saturated Charlie's tan shirt and faded blue jeans. Alexander pulls him back, panicking, trying to find where he is wounded. David searches his legs as Alexander pulls Charlie's shirt up to exam his stomach, then back. Charlie begins to cry. They set him on the snowy ground as Xavier and Milo rush to his side.

They lean down and hover over Charlie, searching frantically to find where he has been hit. "Let me look at him," Milo says. Their search bears nothing. Confused, Alexander looks up to Norma.

Norma collapses. "Mom," Alexander calls out quickly, leaving Charlie's side and rushing to Norma to find the source of the blood. He discovers one of the bullets that the gunmen fired, while she ran for cover to shield Charlie, has deeply wounded her stomach. She was without Kevlar. Her saturated black clothes had hidden her error.

Milo scrambles to her, then David. David sits on the cold ground, removes her headset, and places her head on his lap. He is now pale as panic and fear riddle his face. Tears fill the well of his blood-strained eyes while his nightmare comes to life. Xavier pushes Alexander and Milo to the side.

"Move," he yells. He stabs near her heart and empties a vial of TRH. Dressings pack deep inside the gushing hole while his hands soon warm with her blood. She grows weaker as her skin shivers blue. Xavier slips the needle in and pushes the IV liquid into her veins.

"Alexander," Norma whispers.

Alexander goes to the other side of her as Xavier works, determined to give TRH time to heal her. He kneels. "Mom… I'm here," he says, holding her hand by her side as the other gently strokes her head.

"Son." Norma turns her head to look into Alexander's eyes. She stares deep. Alexander can't take it. He looks away. "Look at me, son." He turns and his face crumbles. "Those eyes are my strength…I am so proud of you! This baby is so lucky." She gasps for air as breaths struggle. Her eyes plead to him. "Tell my grandbaby…tell him…I love him as I love his father...without end…This is all I ever wanted, Alexander." The gasping starts to slow. "Teach him to be strong… Have a heart like yours … to be like you."

Alexander's words begin to fall apart. "No. You tell him. He needs you to teach him!" Norma attempts to rise. "Stay down," he begs.

Norma is too weak. Her shoulders fall flat. She looks to David. "Get old trusty." His hand slides under her shirt, then he slides the knife out from under back. He places it in her trembling hand. Norma tries to lift it, but her strength is waning fast. She looks to Alexander. "Take it. You are ready." Alexander refuses. "Take it!" He removes it from her icy hand, then uses the other to hold on to her tight.

Charlie runs and pushes Alexander to lie on Norma's side. His little arm wraps her neck tight as he cries. Norma turns her head to face him. "Don't cry. This is not your fault…I'm so happy that I found you…" Norma fades and the words stop. Milo gently picks Charlie up to remove him from Norma's side.

"Come here, little buddy. Let them help her," he softly says. He takes him to where the other children are huddled behind Atropos, shielding them from more despair.

"Mom!" Alexander cries out.

Norma wakes, opening her eyes to the Atropos team circling around her. "My men. Atropos, we are victorious. You have served me well." She leans her head back for one more chance to look deep into David's eyes. "You have wasted too much time on me, old friend …but oh how I love you…find someone worthy of you. Love her as you have loved me." Norma's eyes roll back, then reappear, fighting for more time. "Hand me my headset, please." David takes the headset from the ground and places it on her head. Her bloody hand trembles, reaching up to turn it on. David grabs her hand and kisses it, then presses it on for her.

Her voice breaks as she calls for Donovan. "You salty old ass. They finally got me. Watch over my guys!" A slight chuckle releases from her lips as she listens to Donovan. A faint smile drips blood down from the side of her mouth. "And the task I gave you?" Contented eyes and wider smile come across her face hearing of Sarah's progress since Donovan moved her. "She will do well there. Please make sure of it." Norma chokes, then splatters blood onto the headset mic. "*Me quoque.*"

Xavier, kneeling by Norma's side, works his hands inside her stomach, trying desperately to stop the bleeding. He is covered in her blood. For the first time she sees him completely unhinged. "You fat bastard. I always knew you secretly wanted to get your hands on me." She looks as Xavier panics. A droplet lands on Xavier's cheek, and she doubts it's the light snowflakes that are falling. Norma can never recall seeing Xavier cry. "Good God, you do look like a lumberjack. Shave that ugly face," she says, trying to calm his frenzied nerves by using the weapon Xavier uses most in precarious times.

"You're going to be fine." Xavier refuses to give up. Soon the TRH will kick in and she will stand, chastising him. Norma reaches down and softly places her hand on Xavier's blood-drenched arm.

"Xavier…Look at me…Look at me! Vow to me that you will protect the baby to the depths of hell!" Norma moans as the death rattle sounds. "Promise me!"

Xavier breaks down, losing all restraint while his hands persist as she weakens. "I promise," he weeps. Norma pulls his hands out from within her stomach. There is nothing more he can do for her by the amount of warm blood melting the snow.

Alexander brushes her raven hair from her angelic face. "Mom," he calls. Norma only feels the pain from Alexander's eyes. "Mom!"

"Son…I am so tired." Norma calms as she looks to the gray sky, staring into snowflake prisms that are falling down onto her face. No longer does she hear the banshee's whispers. She sighs, never feeling such peace.

"Mom! Don't give up. The TRH will work." His tears fall, dropping onto her face as a single tear escapes her eye, running down the side of her soft pale face. He grips her hand tighter, refusing to let go.

Norma can now see Alex clearly. His beautiful smile, splendid blue eyes; she sighs as she sees his hand reaching for her to take it. "*Amica mea*," she cries. "I want to be with your father now." Drifting to Alex, ready to rejoin her one true love. "How I have missed him."

"No," he howls loudly into the air. Alexander pushes David back and away. He lifts and cradles her into his arms, rocking her to wake. Xavier and David fight to free Alexander from Norma. Alexander swings violently, refusing to let his mother go. Atropos men rally for Alexander to let Norma go now. "No!"

"Let me get her into the helicopter," Xavier yells. Alexander moves as Xavier quickly picks her up, then runs with her draped over his arms. He runs fast… faster.

CHAPTER 34

Alexander rushes to the doors of his penthouse building juggling a paper bag full of grocery list items Nyx had sent him on a mission to retrieve. He has been hustling and dodging DC locals and lost tourists leisurely walking on the hot sidewalks soaking up the summer heat. Beads of sweat drip down his face. Nyx has been frantic to make sure this birthday party was perfect, and with the ingredients within the bag, this Greek dinner will surely be a culinary delight. After all, how often does one celebrate fifty years around the sun—this sun that's been glowing so bright all day? Alexander and Nyx feel this milestone deserves a grand celebration. He thinks that with all that Atropos is—knife wounds, gunshots, broken bones—this should be wonderful indeed.

As he reaches for the handle, he hears his name called out. Alexander turns to see a welcoming face. Mr. Henry ambles along toward him as fast as his feeble feet allow. Alexander smiles, bursting a ray that outshines the sun above. "Mr. Henry," Alexander says, so elated to see him. He shifts the groceries to his left arm to extend a warm hand. Mr. Henry sighs as he attempts to straighten his hunching back. Alexander's heart fills seeing his old friend but marvels how well this old man looks. "How are you?"

"Oh, I can't complain," Mr. Henry says.

"What are you doing here?" Alexander asks.

"I have someone…persistent to meet you." Mr. Henry goes to the corner of the building and waves to the woman and girl standing impatiently. The girl, sweet-faced, breaks free from the woman's hand and runs, swishing her pony tail. Her lanky short legs sprint until barreling over Alexander. Her arms barely wrap him. She squeezes Alexander tight. "Well, hello. What's your name?" Alexander asks.

"This is my granddaughter Olivia. She's been fussing to come meet you. Ms. Olivia here turned ten today," Mr. Henry says. Olivia's mother joins Mr. Henry's side, raising her eyes to look at Alexander. Her look of gratitude appears overwhelming to her. She bashfully smiles, showing to be as happy to meet Alexander as is Olivia. "And this is my daughter Lyla."

"Mr. Alexander, I can't tell you enough how thankful I am for everything you have done for us. Olivia would not be here today if not for you." Her eyes strain as she chokes, trying to remain composed. "We are ever so thankful," Lyla says. Her hand rises to shake the hand responsible for saving her daughter.

Alexander pulls her in close, avidly expressing that Mr. Henry was family to him; therefore she, too, was his family. "There is no need to thank me. Your father has sent plenty of cards and baskets full of my favorites. My pantry has stayed stocked for the past five years since he retired," he says. Alexander bends down to face Olivia. "Your grandfather is very special to me, which makes you special to me as well. If you ever need anything, you make sure your mom or grandfather let me know. Deal?" Alexander motions that a fist pump will seal the deal. Olivia giggles and taps her small fist into Alexander's big knuckles. As Alexander rises, a bottle of oregano falls to the ground. He places it back into the bag and reminds himself that even if he wishes for more time, there is a birthday party that will soon commence. Good manners were in order, seeing Olivia was also having a much celebrated day. She has long exceeded the doctors' original prognosis. "Nyx and I are hosting a much-deserved fiftieth birthday party. Would you like to join us? We would be honored to have you," he says.

"Oh no, Mr. Alexander, that is very gracious of you, but it's best we get on our way. We don't want to bother you anymore."

"Nonsense," Alexander says.

"Maybe another time soon," Lyla says. She reaches in for one more chance to show the fullness in her heart and hugs Alexander. Olivia steals a moment as well.

"We best be goin'," Mr. Henry says as he gestures that it's time for the two ladies to leave Alexander to his party.

Alexander watches as his old friend, Lyla, and Olivia walk away. Olivia quickly spins around and runs back to Alexander. She wraps his legs for one more time before leaving him.

"Mr. Alexander...you're special to me, too," she says while buckteeth appear from such a lovely smile.

"Honey, I'm home," Alexander yells as he uses his foot to swing the door shut.

"Hey, buttercup," David says, coming to Alexander's aid to take the grocery bag from his arms and place it into the kitchen.

"Is the birthday honoree here?" Alexander asks.

Nyx comes from the kitchen and raises tiptoed to give Alexander a hello kiss just as she has since the day they were married and she moved in. "Not yet," she says, wiping her wet hands dry with a dish towel.

One by one, Lander, Kosmo, Stefen, Vali, Milo, and Nick pour out from the kitchen with aromas of Greek fusions wafting behind them. Donovan slowly follows as his cane clanks on the wood floor. Each carries a glass of bourbon poured neat. Just as they always have for such an occasion. "I see you all wasted no time to break into my mom's private stock. That was for me, you dickheads—" He's interrupted.

"Alexander," Nyx scolds, then chuckles. It has been a task the past few years for her to rid the room of profanities whenever Atropos gathers around. "You boys," Nyx says, playfully swatting Alexander on the butt with the dishtowel.

The men gather around the couch, jabbing with witty banter as they wait for the knock on the door. Tales can be heard loudly, then whispers, followed by an abrupt "Asshole!" Nyx can hear David and Donovan hushing the men whenever excitable voices become too loud.

"You're going to wake up Norma," David says. Norma has been napping in the nearby room, fighting a summer cold.

A light knock raps on the door. Alexander jumps to his feet to answer. "Look who decided to show up for their own birthday. Whoa, what did you do to your face? I can't believe you shaved!"

Xavier bull rushes in, pushing Alexander to the side. "Move, sweet cheeks. What Norma wants, Norma gets," he says. Xavier scans the room. "Where is she?" he asks.

"Whipped," Alexander says.

Noises begin to wrestle awake as coughs rattle in the other room. The guys rise to their feet as Alexander heads for the door to help her out. Before his hand can take hold of the handle, the door swings wildly open. Raven locks bounce as swift feet move cheerfully toward Xavier. A grin like no other comes across Xavier's face.

"Uncle Xavier," Norma calls out, running past her father to jump into Xavier's wide, opened arms.

"There's my girl," Xavier says.

"Happy birt-day," she sings, the sweetest sounds Xavier's ears have ever heard. Little arms wrap tightly around his broad neck. Snot bubbles pop from her nose. Xavier uses his sleeve to wipe her nose clean, then kisses her angelic cheek. Norma takes her tiny hand and strokes Xavier's face. "No more itchies. You did it for me?" she asks, giggling.

A sweet yet painful feeling hits Alexander in the chest. "I wish Mom and Dad could've seen this." Nyx walks to Alexander's side and puts her comforting arm around his waist. "This little girl turns that big hard clump into mush," Alexander says. Nyx smiles and comments how their little Norma has Xavier wrapped so tightly around her tiny finger. "I don't think we have to worry about her being protected." He can see his parents looking down at little Norma, smiling.

"Uncle Xavier, I a warrior," Norma says, pretending to chop chop him down.

"No sweetie… you're my raven-haired princess. I am *your* warrior," he says, poking her tummy to make her giggle.

David takes his glass off the table, and soon the rest follow. As they traditionally have on every occasion since Norma's death, they toast to honor their fallen Atropos leader. Glasses rise high. "To Norma," he honors. The Atropos men roar: "To Norma!"

"To me!" little Norma yells as she raises her sippy cup, spilling juice down her and Xavier's shirts. David steals Norma from Xavier's arms and tickles her cheek with his face. She laughs silly.

"You come to *pa-poosch*," David says. He places her cup on the coffee table and wipes her shirt with a napkin.

"Pa-poo, I love you." Norma presses her small lips together and kisses David on his cheek. Her little arms span out to grab Xavier and pull him in for a shared hug. "I love you, too, Uncle Xavier," she says, tickled pink that all her favorite guys are here with her now. David hands back her sippy cup. "Atopos, Atopos," her sugary voice sings.

"Not yet," Alexander says.

"Not ever," Nyx says.

"*Donec mors nos separaverit*," they shout. "To Norma!"

In writing this book, my research led me to learning more about the bravery and humanity of organizations that are within the United States and our government that are committed to ending the atrocities depicted in this book. These acts of savagery against our children must end.

"Slavery is alive and well in the land of free," could not be truer.

An excerpt from The United State Department of Justice:

"Some of our most vulnerable children also face the threat of being victimized by commercial sexual exploitation. Runaways, throwaways, sexual assault victims, and neglected children can be recruited into a violent life of forced prostitution." —Deputy Attorney General James Cole speaking at the National Strategy Conference on Combating Child Exploitation in San Jose, California, May 17, 2011.

Child trafficking happens in our own backyard, to our neighbors, and our children's friends from school. It's been shown that at-risk youth are particularly vulnerable targets for traffickers, but other children simply are at risk from unsupervised online access to social media outlets used to seek approval. No one is immune to becoming a victim of trafficking; if your child has access to the internet, then they are at risk. If they have private access to the internet inside of their bedrooms, it is equivalent to a window left open to be victimized. Keep in mind, traffickers are experts at exploiting children's vulnerabilities and can lure a child away from your home without using force.

Who are these children? Are they runaways, homeless, and orphans? The truth is that traffickers don't discriminate as to whom they choose to target. Trafficking occurs in suburbs, urban, poor, and rural areas.

What happens to a child once they've been forced into a child trafficking situation? Some are immediately put on airplanes and sent to foreign countries. Many times the money generated is used to fund terrorist organizations as depicted in this book. Others are sent to meet the demands in cities and states around the United States. Trafficking stolen children to other areas helps traffickers avoid the possibility of the children being recognized locally through amber alerts, media, and/or police barricades. As a result, many traffickers operate near metropolitan airports and other transportation hubs where they can take a child and flee miles away within minutes.

What happens once outside the United States? These children are forced into child labor, sex camps, or have organs harvested, then never found.

As stated, it is not solely in the United States where this occurs. Taken from Glenn Beck's website: By 2014, ISIS captured, murdered, and human sex and labor trafficked Christians and ethno-religious minorities in the region of its self-proclaimed Islamic state. By 2015, a population of over 3 million people was reduced to 300,000. On August 28, 2015, Glenn Beck leads the charge at the "Restoring Unity" event in Birmingham, Alabama. It is after that he brings to the forefront through his radio show about the atrocities that were being committed by the terrorist group Islamic State, referring it to as the "Christian Holocaust." In September 2015, The Nazarene Fund (TNF) was formed and on December 10, 2015, the first operation was conducted to rescue 149 Christian refugees from Iraq safely into Slovakia, their new home. March 2016, The Nazarene Fund goes deep into ISIS territory in Syria to rescue the Younan family. Their father was murdered and the mother, with four daughters at foot, was on the run and being hunted. The Younan mother and children were rescued in a The Nazarene Fund operation during the middle of the night. They had to travel through twenty-eight checkpoints before the family would arrive safely in Lebanon. By June 2016, The Nazarene Fund had rescued and restored 272 families, totaling 1,100 lives. March 2018, The Nazarene Fund was on the ground in Syria performing reconnaissance missions, with operatives working with the The Nazarene Fund assisting in saving Christians and Yazidis from human trafficking or organ harvesting that is commonly happening throughout

Syria to fund terrorism. Although defeated, the ISIS threat is still very real to the persecuted minorities of the region as well as to the thousands of captives and slaves under its control.

Adding another vile chapter to its dark history, ISIS and some of its former members are now involved in the international slave trade and organ harvesting and trafficking markets as depicted in this novel.

In this novel, Charlie is found; in reality, too many are never returned.

On January 31, 2020, President Trump signed an Executive Order on combating human trafficking and online child exploitation in the United States.

It is my wish that this novel brings to light the reality and dangers of child trafficking with hopes to one day end and ultimately destroy this roughly $150 billion a year business for child traffickers.